TIME TO FALL

TIME TO FALL

A Novella

AUSTIN C. BEAL

RESOURCE *Publications* • Eugene, Oregon

TIME TO FALL
A Novella

Resource Publications
An Imprint of Wipf and Stock Publishers
199 W. 8th Ave., Suite 3
Eugene, OR 97401

www.wipfandstock.com

PAPERBACK ISBN: 978-1-7252-6567-7
HARDCOVER ISBN: 978-1-7252-6566-0
EBOOK ISBN: 978-1-7252-6568-4

Manufactured in the U.S.A.   06/25/20

To Wanda, to Luda, to the Old Man in the drive.

To Dickens, to Lewis, and to all the fore-read no longer alive.

To all those who wander, contending to survive.

And to my wife, to whom I owe the work of my life.

Memory, oh, memory, oh, how it wanes;
Memory, oh, memory, oh, how it fades;
Memory, oh, memory, oh, how it pains,
That I can only remember,
The memory of you and your charades.

Contents

I

Band on a Ring

BENEATH SKY AND CLOUD, under metal and mortar, under all things, I stood at my post before the podium, awaiting the end of my shift. The day was just beginning to fade into early evening. The sun and its blades cut through the trees behind me creating an odd mixture of light and shade beneath the driveway overhang which swept up into a ramp from the second floor of the hospital. Lines of light and shadow danced like piano keys mid-concerto as a rush of wind rustled alive the forest, welcoming the approaching fall.

In time, an old brown Town Car rattled around the corner and into the parkway. I ripped a ticket and prepared to assist the driver. The car came to a stop just past my station. An old man, skinny and frail looking, exited the shabby vehicle, cane in hand. The man wore a white mustache, a firmly pressed plaid shirt—tucked—and a rugged looking pair of denims fitted properly high. His cane, mahogany of some sort, looked astonishingly polished with a thick lacquer and was adorned with a golden eagle at the head end. His shoes—brown, new, untarnished, and undoubtedly orthopedic—matched his belt and cane, yet nothing of his appearance matched the car he drove. His vehicle matched only his visibly all-but-defeated spirit and, perhaps, his age, counterbalancing the manner in which he dressed and groomed. I thought this an enigma, one of little consequence of course; though, in consequence, I now thought him enigmatic.

"That'll be four dollars, sir," I said, extending the valet ticket toward him.

"Very well, then . . . *Charlie*," agreed the old man, inspecting my nametag at an otherwise uncomfortably close distance. Proceeding, he reached into his billfold and presented four wrinkled singles.

"Thank you, sir. We're here till eight this evening. I'll have it pulled right up front for you."

"Thank you, son. I shouldn't be long."

The old man handed me his keys and hobbled off inside to his appointment. His was the only car parked at this hour, so I didn't bother hanging them. Instead, I set them atop the podium and stared off through the hospital windows, watching the old man limp leisurely into the elevator. Looking down again, I inspected the old man's keys. Nothing terribly interesting: a miniature Swiss Army knife, a leather swatch adorned with an unrecognizable emblem, and several room keys, from what it appeared, recalling to mind in shape and number those which hung from the belt of a janitor. I noticed a metal band which spun on the keyring when turning them over, a peculiar item to carry around in that way, I thought. It was dull and worn, looking as if time had not displaced, but merely hidden a once vibrant luster. "How dull it is to pause, to make an end. To rust unburnish'd, not to shine in use!" I pondered, recollecting Lord Tennyson's Ulysses, so different from the Ulysses of myth and legend.

I dropped the keys in the top drawer and wandered off to pace and plan and think, as all young men do, and to wait.

◆ ◆ ◆

Half-past eight and the old man had yet to return for his car. On the bench where I now sat, I could see a spider weaving its web for the night. In the misery of waiting, I imagined it would grow in size and stature and swallow me here whole alive under the rising moon that I may die by a kinder predator than silent boredom. Was it true that boredom was only desire seeking desire? At that moment I sought the desire for something, yes, something like a story.

At last I heard the hospital doors glide open. I roused to my feet, turning to the podium. Ticket in hand, the old man gradually made his way toward me.

"Is this mine?" he said in a tired tone, looking perplexed as he gestured with a gaze toward the brown Town Car, unmoved from its arrival.

"Yes, it is, sir. Don't you recognize it?"

He paused.

"If I could only remember," he muttered under his breath. "There's a mystery to memory, son; one I haven't yet mastered."

I chucked wryly, perplexed by the weight of his sentiment. I pulled his keys from the drawer. The band slid into the side of my finger as I held out the set toward their rightful owner. I felt compelled to ask the old man about the ring, thinking it a talisman or some novelty bearing with it a story, perhaps. I proceeded to inquire.

"Will you tell me, sir, what is this ring on your keys?" I asked in wonder, in curiosity, meeting the old man's eyes with a lively look.

The old man sighed heavily as his countenance seemed to slump into a submission of sadness. His shoulders, held so nearly high just a moment ago, now drooped deeper into a shrug.

"That's a long story, son. Have you the time?" he asked, with a new twinkle in his eyes, returning to me the favor of my hopeful gaze as his shoulders shifted back and his posture erected.

Almost out of duty or an inherent respect for my elder, or in that sense of intrigue which is to most of my kind irresistible, I obliged to listen despite the time, hoping all the while that my hope for a story was met with a consideration for brevity at the thought of a young man's want for supper at an hour before too late. We would see. I agreed with a nod.

The old man and I moved to sit on the same bench behind the podium which overlooked a retention area. I brushed away the spider's web as we sat. An egret waltzed down toward the water as the light of the moon, rising higher to its post in the night sky, shown out from behind the hospital.

I looked intently at the old man, awaiting his story. Age shown through his furrowed visage, greater now under the mix of

3

moonbeam and the unflattering fluorescence of the exterior hospital lighting. He spoke. His voice, deeper and more dream-like, echoed in the driveway and over the pond and through time itself as he recalled this tale:

"In the time I spent in the Orient, days or decades, I cannot place it, I learned precisely how to panic. That day, I awoke above a small, inconspicuous tavern just south of Ban Mo. There were two bunks in the slummy one-room flat, mine and one also inhabited on the opposing wall to my right. Between us, a poorly hewn and stained dark wood floor that had seen the better part of its life already—chipped and creaking under foot, with lumps and dips to waiver faith in its integrity at each step—marked off a chasm I thought impassable in the stillness of that waking moment.

As my eyes adjusted to the light of morning, I made out the form of a slender, tan, freckled upper-back and shoulders of what I imagined to be a beautiful young woman asleep in that adjacent bunk. Her head faced the outer wall, resting on a pillow with her arms tucked beneath. The sheets, below her back, covered the remainder of civilization, save for her toes, exposed off the end of the too-short cot. She flinched slightly and strands of her long, golden hair drifted across her back. Her head began to turn slowly toward me. As her back arched, slipping the covers from their stay, her arms reached forward like a cat stretching awake under the sun about a safer floor on any lazy Sunday afternoon. I quickly pretended to sleep, listening intently for an assurance that she hadn't awoken entirely.

After a short period of silence, when no further rustling could be heard from my presumed companion's bunk, I haltingly opened my eyes. To my surprise, the bunk was empty. I sat up—a creak of the floor—and found her again to my right, standing by the window. The sunlight poured in, falling over what I could see of her body, veiled now by a white nightgown. Given the manner in which she stood—contrapposto leaning against the casement—I could see only her silhouette, for the entirety of her form was shadowed also in waves by the sheer curtain which ruffled over her just then as a cool breeze eased over the sill of the open window.

From that window, by which it seemed the world itself might be looking in, she turned slow and graceful. Facing me, her eyes—hazel, amber, or emerald—I could not tell from the distance, seemed anyway to shift shades, flickering reflections of the sunlight outside. They glowed regardless: bright, joyful, and spontaneous. Her whole being glowed. She was something out of a dream—a vision through the dusty light of that ancient tavern loft. Her mere presence, in that light or any, it seemed, shifted the atmosphere from an aura of decay, even shame, to that of new life, even hope, a word I had not heard or spoke of or thought in a long time. Another breeze eased in, waving fibers of gilded hair across her face. She cleared the strands to one side, setting them behind her ear, and spoke . . .

"Good morning, Captain. Did you sleep well?"

II

Thailand

BRUCE

A KNOCK AT THE door rushed me to my feet. Unintelligible Thai chattered from the other side, from the mouth of an obviously angry master of the house.

"It's alright, dear," the woman reassured me.

"*Dear*?" I thought.

I shouted something back at the man outside, in broken Thai of course, and after a moment's silence, footsteps were heard moving down the stairs.

"We might have outstayed our welcome, Jack," she said sweetly.

"*Jack*," I thought. "May-be," I replied.

"What's say we fly this place and have some real fun, in the city," she said, beaming.

There was no saying *no* to that face, to those eyes, which seemed to have life in them for a nation.

"Alright," I said with an ease and a contentment then foreign to me. "Nothing for me here, anyway. Seems the landlord has it in his mind to throw me out already."

"Nothing for '*us*' here, indeed," the woman said coyly as she, with some effort, pulled up a pair of jeans I hadn't noticed lying on the floor, and with no apparent effort, completed the look, put up

6

her hair and, upon her wrists, a watch and bracelets, and finally, rings on her fingers.

"Here," she said, tossing me my shirt. "Put this on, Rambo. Don't want you causing any more locals to stumble, now do we?"

"'We'? . . . 'Us'?" I pondered inwardly, confused at the presumptuous possessives.

"Very well, then. Topless no longer," I answered, staring at her back as she sat before the tiny, rusted, and faded mirror which leaned precariously atop an otherwise tiny dresser that she must have drawn closer to the end of her bunk the night previous, putting on what makeup she didn't need. "Does she realize I'll be gone by sundown?" I thought to myself. "Still . . ."

I didn't at first notice the glance she gave out of the corner of that spotted mirror as she brushed her eyelash, a look as though she knew otherwise, like she knew my scheme and her counter to it, as if she were a step—or ten—ahead of my planned departure. She told me of it later, you see, of all the glances in all the worlds she gave to me. She kept none for herself.

"Wait, wait, wait," I interrupted. "What do you mean, 'She told me later'? I thought . . ."

"Quiet, son! I'm only liable to get through this once. And you're lucky if that!"

"Alright, alright . . . go on."

"Yes, where was I?"

"You've got a shirt on now, I think . . ."

"Indeed . . ."

We, *I*, I mean, I packed my single shoulder bag, she grabbed her purse, and we were off: down the creaking stairs—worse than the floor, if you can imagine it—through the tavern, and out into that muggy street. The sun had moved behind the clouds now, though. What was blinding through the open window was now tamed and shut up outside. But nothing could tame that Oriental humidity.

I hadn't any idea of any named "city" near that tavern, but she seemed to know the way. I only followed my nose in these parts, at these times, and wherever we were heading was the obvious choice for what interested me most at that moment: food, street food.

"Hungry?" she asked with her omniscient air, which would've annoyed me more if she weren't so stunning carrying it.

"She'll be a hard one to escape," I thought, I was sure of it. "Yes, quite so," I answered. We turned a corner, down a market street where the smells overwhelmed the senses: Oyster Mee Sua, Oyster Omelette, Lu Rou Fan, Beef Noodles, the gambit in this grotto. She made for anything oyster, and I, for the Beef Noodles, where I felt safest.

We carried our delicacies, mine in my left hand, hers in her right. The whole time she walked just behind me, I noticed, her left hand looking all the while like it was trying not to rise up and grab my arm, caress my back, or simply and shyly take my hand. I felt nervous, uncomfortable, and the feeling made me remember that I carried something else in every city and in every town: the sky, the memory of what I wanted to forget. "Spirits in the head," I think they've been called.

She stopped at a vendor's cart to browse what woodworks, scarfs, and trinkets were on display, the same junk in every city it seemed. I drifted as casually as I could to the other side of the street, pretending to shop as well—easy enough—then I slipped into a corner alley and made my escape.

I didn't realize she was watching over her shoulder. What was it I heard her say through the chatter of that street?

"Time to fall, Bruce . . ."

But I was already gone, alighting from alley to alley, street to street, then at a corner, mounting a rickshaw to the airfield, and I didn't even ask her name.

III

London

THE WOMAN

I DREAMT THAT NIGHT on the plane to Heathrow. It was an old story, I think, a recurring dream for me at any rate. Ironic, or was it comedic? The real question, was it his destiny or mine, that Appointment in Samarra? The story in my head revolved in the same way at each interval. The Speaker is always Death, and here is Her tale which circled in my dreams:

> There was a merchant in Baghdad who sent his servant to market to buy provisions. In a little while, the servant came back, white and trembling, and said, "Master, just now when I was in the marketplace I was jostled by a woman in the crowd, and when I turned, I saw it was Death that jostled me. She looked at me and made a threatening gesture. Now, lend me your horse and I will ride away from this city and avoid my fate. I will go to Samarra and there, Death will not find me."
>
> The merchant lent him his horse, the servant mounted it, and digging his spurs into its flanks, off he went as fast as the horse could gallop. A little later, the merchant went to the marketplace and saw me standing in the crowd. He approached me and said, "Why did you

make a threatening gesture to my servant when you saw him this morning?"

"That was not a threatening gesture," I said, "It was only a start of surprise. I was astonished to see him in Baghdad, for I had an appointment with him tonight, in Samarra."

I awoke as the plane was landing, with the same afterthought. The story—a bit morbid—but it was as intriguing as when he first told it to me. I knew of several individuals in our camp who were more keen on that kind of predestination than they should be, though I fancied the idea too, in that way at least, the literary way, a sort of storied whimsy so opposed to actual application. It was the same fancy I maintained for what other theology Bruce taught me. Something about a "redemptive abandonment" came to mind now, though I always wondered in the same vein if that were anything prescriptive for us, humans, I mean. It seems the other pursuit, the unwavering kind, was the more humane. I've heard there is a love as strong as Her, as the Speaker, Death, I mean, a love always meant for us to have and to do unto. "All were in play now," I thought. Three or four more moves to one endgame or the other—to love or death, come what may.

The plane touched down with a jolt and I saw the back of his head four rows up to my right. It was so like him, needing his neck shaved, and no one to tell him. What a shame. We taxied to the terminal gate. I sunk down a bit for him not to see me. My face flushed; my stomach turned. I watched him pull his grey duffle bag from at his feet, grabbed my purse, and tailed him, five or so persons back, through the skybridge. In the terminal I waded into the sea of people and watched him and his unkempt neck move with intent toward some bar somewhere. One man among so many, and so easy to see. They were together like Mr. Pound's "petaled people," but crowded on a silver bow of the same existence, though in Bruce's mind all were indistinguishable corollas, forgotten at first glance, or melded together in one continuous look upon similitude as one might take in a meadow at speed at a distance. But I could always find him. He stood out to me like a rose among thorns, like a bear swimming in a tank of fishes—a grizzly in a pool, or perhaps, in an aquarium. How silly. With all his imagined training, it was quite easy following him too. But what was I thinking? It really was all only ever in his head, that tradecraft of a different sort, of which he was at present oblivious.

Bruce finally found what he wanted in an airport lounge: a peaceful place of solitude, with quiet and disinterested company that would pay him no mind. He was never really in it for the drink. Within, only two other souls were present: an off-duty pilot—we hope—in a booth by a floor-to-ceiling window, and the barkeep. I stood on the threshold just outside the entry door, an automatic door, that is, which kept opening and shutting right in front of me, to my chagrin and, quite frankly, nervous embarrassment, which doubled at every opening whereby I was met with the barkeep's perplexed glances. "He must be new," I thought.

Shaking that feeling, my heart raced again, as it did each time, surprisingly, in anticipation. And now, in flowed a flurry of school-girl excitement mixed with a hope so stubborn that it would endure a thousand of these pursuits in the course of this life, till that other world repaired all the damage done, putting things to rights, as they say.

I pulled up my skirt—just a tad, mind you; not even an inch, really, and only for a moment, relinquishing to the truth that he would not recognize or even perceive any kind of "unfading beauty" in his condition, though he would prefer it if he knew it—puckered my lips, primped my hair and walked placidly but purposefully in, taking my seat, two from him, looking as detached but attractive, as disinterested but accessible, and as innocent but experienced as I knew how. I caught his eye and the hunt was over before it began . . .

"Uhh, question, please," I interrupted, politely raising my hand this time. "So, *she's* telling the story now, right?"

"Yes, yes, of course," the old man said. "It is better that you hear it from her side here, and elsewhere perhaps, so you might know how she thought throughout."

"Okay, okay, just checking. Please, do go on."

"Alright, fine. Now, where was I?"

"The hunt . . ."

"Ah, yes . . ."

11

◆ ◆ ◆

THE ABBEY

"Where you headed, soldier?" I called from down the bar. "Oh!" I thought, kicking myself. "He's not supposed to know I know that, or, think that. Never mind."

"To the only place worth seeing here," he said soberly.

"Where's that? The Eye?" I exclaimed, nearly discharging my tonic through my nose in a gasped attempt not to laugh at my own quip.

"No," he said chuckling, "But that's clever. I'm headed into the west, to the church of churches, the Abbey of abbeys, Westminster Abbey, that is," he said in that smooth, rhythmic, professorial voice, cocking his head just a little to his right and turning up his eyebrows, as was his custom.

"Mmhmm, *you're* clever," I replied, thinking, "Who's hunting who? Or was it *whom*?"

"Do you know what the name means? Westminster?" he asked me. I could have sworn he had once told me.

"Ministers in the west?" I said, turning up a question. "That can't be right."

"No, no," he said, graciously shaking his head and chuckling again. "It hasn't any real meaning like that. Westminster is just the city's name, a town or a borough, something like that, within the greater London. Wouldn't have the same ring to it for boroughs and towns in the States, now would it?"

"I suppose not," I said, smiling at him with an admiration that didn't need any supplement, but rather a reigning in, for I could tell it carried with it in tone and even posture a supreme effort at mere affectation, trying only to give off an air of patriotic comradery, and not an aged affection, which was the actual tinged emotion I so obviously felt at that moment. The experience might compare to anyone meeting their hero or their idol, their star or their crush, or even their long-lost lover or their perpetually prodigal person, wanting to withhold the immense emotions that such a reuniting might conjure.

"It was once called Thorn Ey, the 'Ey' sounding the same *I* without the 'e.' So you might have been half right, or, at least a third, in pronunciation." He smiled, paused, looked down at his glass, then up again, opening his posture toward me as he spun on his stool. "Care to join me?"

"Why, y-yes. I-I'd like that," stuttering awkwardly, almost shyly. "Shall we?" I replied coolly, recovering, gesturing with my eyes toward that silly, sliding automatic door, feeling as nervous and as excited as when I first stood before it. We were off, out that door, through the terminals, and into the west we hurried, to make Evensong. I, filled with joy, *overflowed* with hope again as he opened the cab door, ushering me in. It wouldn't be long now; I could sense it. *Compelle intrare.* He would come.

We talked small and large and even deep in the cab. We joked and laughed with the driver too. I always loved hearing their accents, his from somewhere north, I thought, Middlesbrough perhaps, the end of the line it seemed, that city, but not a long train ride from where we now traveled. We worked with orphans there one summer. Back then, departing the train at our connection on a journey further up and further in country, we had so many bags and were in such a hurry, he pulled someone else's luggage from the shelves, thinking it our own. We would laugh at that too now, if he would, well, you know. And he would doubly laugh at the thought of those eclectic but so appropriate "Caution Wet Floor" signs we would always notice, shaped like upside-down peeling bananas, which littered the Underground. What minds men have, to make merry the mundane.

Traffic stopped near Buckingham Palace and we saw the reason: a parade of horses with riders in full color guard, carrying staffs and banners, trotted ceremoniously down the park side of the palace. The gold on their hats glinted in the afternoon sunlight as the white of their gloves and uniforms gleamed as bright as any singular summer cloud or snow-capped mountain I had ever seen. The old soldiers were picturesque Britannia, I thought, in that light or any, marching in sequenced solemnity before the backdrop of that sublime greenery draped in yellow tulips which clothed the park surface behind them. Or were they azaleas? The trumpet sounded.

13

"Take us around the circle, please, sir," he said to the cabby. "Shall we try and see the Queen?"

"Yes! Oh, yes!" I exclaimed, wrapping my arm in his, pulling him a bit too hard and a bit too close, I thought. But he didn't seem to mind. We stopped at the front gates, jumped out the cab and, weaving between the passers-by, slipped through the other tourists, all with their phones and cameras held high, to nestle into the perfect space between the hinges of the right-side gate as it was opening toward us.

I watched the procession of horses behind us now, marching down out of sight. As I turned back again toward the swinging gates, "There she is!" I whispered in rapture. She passed us slowly, seated still and waving natural, smiling cheerful but serious from the backseat of that exquisite green Bentley. Or was it a Rolls Royce? He would know. Yes, there she was—the Queen of England in all her stoic but kind-eyed, regal-hatted glory. What would it be like, to be Queen for a day? Was it terribly cliché to wonder? And was she really a figurehead or a proper monarch of old? What sway did she still hold in this land? Quite a lot still, I imagined, at least with public opinion, given the shouts and jeers that surrounded us at that moment. But these were his thoughts now, I noticed, his in mine, and these were tourists, like us.

We hailed another cab, hurried inside, and before long we approached the circle in front of the Abbey just as Evensong was starting. He flung open the cab door, took my hand, and we ran within, shifting shades from happy to solemn as we slowed our run to a quiet pace, masking our glee for the atmosphere of that old church—as regal as the Queen Mother, as holy as the Temple Mount—the Abbey of Ey. We had arrived.

We really did enter at the west door, clever he was, still. We had been here a thousand times it seemed, but the feeling was always the same upon entering that vestibule: of awe, of upward gazing contemplation, then downward facing reflection. We both glanced around as we always did; he, always as if for the first time.

"Is it any wonder we don't build churches like this anymore? Just malls that shape the ground, and towers that scrape the sky, making places for and placing names upon, like Babylon, without

14

any thought to—or knowledge of—that story's end. The more stories, the less substance, I say, when you haven't got enough sense to fill them with anything really lasting," he mused, pontificating. "What good is a race to the heavens when it's run only to get higher and mightier than the neighbors?"

"Mmhm, you're right, dear."

I once heard of a cathedral in our home country, one with the steeple cut off, with a flat roof to signify the infinite and open expansion of knowledge, with no point, I imagined, to point to any Originator of it, because that would narrow or *limit* knowledge, so the thinking went. Quite silly, I thought, to have a war upon theology with the building of a church like that for some other purpose than theological reflection. I imagined there would be quite the dissonance in the mind upon entering that vestibule. Where would or could the eyes be drawn? If up, to what, or to whom? Man is not in the sky. You couldn't even dream as much on the top floor of the tallest skyscraper. "Ah, his thoughts again," I realized. We stopped short in the middle of the hall. Bruce was looking down.

"Ironic, isn't it?" he said.

"What, dear?"

"That *he* is buried just here, in the middle of the hall."

"Who, dear?"

"Darwin. Buried between King Henry's and Queen Elizabeth's of old, between fathers and mothers, soldiers and saints from all sides of Christendom, here lies Darwin, the father of macrobe, I mean, *macro* evolution and the dissension and consequent decline of divine thought, of which he might be singularly to blame. What a legacy, what a place to be laid to rest, in the hall of the thing you nearly brought down."

"Well, he did go to seminary, didn't he? And he is a sort of national hero. Well, at least he's famous, for something, I mean."

"*Infamous* in these halls, at least he should be. Silly, just silly. But never mind that now. Let's catch the choir and be off."

We heard the voices coming in to meet us—in chorus, in canon, in cadence now—the praises bouncing to-and-fro, off the walls and through those storied halls, up and up the sculpted arches, up and up the parapets, up and up and out into the heavens where

Someone sat enthroned upon them all, I was sure of it. "My goodness, there wasn't music like this anywhere back home," I thought.

We quickened our pace to the sanctuary, passing through the nave where little semicircle chapels were cut out into the walls. Communion was being served in one to our left. Within that little alcove we saw the strays and stowaways, the students and the sinners of every day and every age, some seeking and finding, some sitting and forgetting, some standing in faith, and some, some only soldering on in fear, I thought. The ministers seemed to surround us as we neared the music, dressed in their white vestments streaked with red arms and edges, looking so content in their places, moving slowly and solemnly on that checkered floor, like pieces in a game afoot—checkers rather than chess, but with a queen nonetheless. At the usher's nod, we took our seats in a back pew, to listen and to hear.

It was full evening when we stepped outside, where the sun was going down somewhere in the west, and it was high time for food and drink and the telling of tales, I thought. We dined together at the hotel restaurant, the same hotel where we by pure chance were together staying, on the same floor no less, if you can believe it. After dinner, we made the elevator just as the clock struck ten, my face flushing and my stomach fluttering once more. Would he come in again? The bell tolled and the doors eased open to our floor.

"After you, 'my dear,'" he said, with sweet sarcasm. In he would come, a little further this time, stay for a little longer, I hoped.

◆ ◆ ◆

FROM NIGHT, A LIGHT

"Do you, um," I hesitated, facing him between the rooms in the middle of the hall on our floor. "Do you want to come in, perhaps for some tea, an-and some Biscoffs? I nabbed some extras on the plane."

"That would be lovely," he said calmly, smoothly, with an uncanny, stable confidence. "I do love those little cookies, or are they biscuits?"

"Biscottis, I think," I returned coyly, ushering him down the hall, around the corner now, a little further in. "I'm in 427, just here," motioning to my room.

"Ah, capital."

I scanned the key as he opened the door over my shoulder, stepped one foot in, and I felt him grace my lower back with his hand, ushering *me* in now. I looked back at him. He smiled, in a kind, in a loving, but most certainly, in an *interested* manner. The glint in his eyes I had seen before. Merriment was afoot in his mind. I flushed hot, then cold at the same time, for the nerves.

"Tea, then?" I said in anxious anticipation, clearing my throat a bit before the little serving table at the wall as he sat in the armchair behind me.

"Why, yes. No sugar, no anything, please. Just a Biscoff—or two—on the side, of course," he winked.

"Alright, my— . . .," I stopped short, catching myself. "Coming right up."

We sat for tea—and Biscoffs—at a small table by the window which looked out over Trafalgar Square. He told me of the great battle, of the navy, of the Napoleonic War, of the coast and that cape, and about the new statue they were planning in the Square, a tribute to an "Invisible Enemy," they say, made in the shape of an ancient, winged, monstrous idol god.

"How foolish," I thought, to in plain sight put up a religious siege work like that. It would certainly make a statement, though. Perhaps that's what the artist wanted, but I was never a fan of that sort of thing, socio-political-religious patronage. And there is still some wrath reserved for those "breathless idols," ancient or not. What men's hands have made, "worthless idols." They might be taught for . . .

"Are you listening?" Bruce said suddenly.

"Uh . . . yes, yes of course . . . The 'Invisible Enemy,' was it?"

"I'm boring you, aren't I?" he replied shyly, chuckling. "I'm sorry. Enough of the history lesson. Let's talk about you . . ."

17

"I think we've talked enough, for now," I said, leaning in towards him, touching the top of his hand with mine, grazing it up the hair on his arm, turning it in and over, pressing gently, drawing him in and up, awaiting his reaction. He seemed not to mind again. I stood and drew my hand gracefully up and onto his shoulder, then, bending down, pressed my lips soft against his cheek. His arm made its way around me, his hand settling on the small of my back again, moving slowly now, though, *very* slowly, downward. I whispered in his ear, "*Time to fall, Bruce . . .*" He kissed me, long and sweet, and before I could finish, our night began, and was ended.

"Hey! Did they, I mean, did you, and her . . .?!" I cut in, uncontrollably, and "rudely" this time, again, apparently.

"Be decent, boy!" The old man said sharply. "Now, where was I?"

"You and the woman had just . . ." I started, nodding my head in tacit but honest approval, brows raised and smiling.

"Stop that! Yes, yes, the shadow had fallen again, even in that moment, but the light was just breaking through. One more storm to bear now, perhaps two . . ."

When morning came, Bruce was up and getting dressed somewhere in the room. The sheets were cold next to me. I laid on my side in silence, finding him now just around the corner of the entryway wall. I watched him put on his shirt, seeing it catch on his hand inside the elbow sleeve, snickering at how he pretended it didn't happen. What silly pride men have, even when they think no one watches. "What if someone were watching?" must be in their mind's eye all the time. Maybe it should be. Some eyes "roam throughout the earth," keeping watch on one, on all, perhaps. He faced me, working away at his trousers now.

He managed to stay fit since he "left the service," I noticed, gazing at him and his still opened shirt, admiring the shape of him, what I could see of it anyway, what I imagined I remembered of it, and up conjured that old and enduring affection again. I thought of the night, of us, of all things. *It* never really worked toward what I wanted, though, now did it? No, not in this way. Cotton candy to a starved soul, it seemed, still. Was that how it was once put to me? But how was *he* managing? It was so long in between, though

18

he was always better at lasting and fasting than I. "*It* is like cotton candy—fun for a while, but you'll die trying to live by it." That was it, even for us. But at least it caught his attention, for a time anyway.

There must be something more for him now, something more I could give him, of me. "God, why is this happening?!" No, I can't think like that. Not now. I must soldier on. A new day with new mercy cometh on; the dark has nearly drawn. It is as the poet Alexander said:

> ". . . yes, dusk and dust have drawn
> From night a light—forward unto dawn . . ."

"Oh, you're up. Better dress. I have an early checkout," he declared, looking over at me still on the bed, seated up now, arms around my knees.

"Yes, me too," I said, a little in despair.

We left the hotel, side by side but no longer together, not knowing where we walked. On the street, we passed another but younger church, and then another a few blocks down. One barred, two barred, would three of the four parish doors be locked? All appeared that way, shut-up from the inside. Bruce approached one set of them, tugging on the ornate, iron handles.

"Locked." He paused, looking the door up and down. "I wonder if the old gods have any sway here any longer. I wonder what they'd say to this locked door."

"No doors can hold *them*, now can they?" I asked gently but with a resolve to encourage.

"Right . . . If I remember rightly, no locked door held *Him* from that Upper Room, now did it? And He was even 'a little lower than the angels,' was He not? Yes, I thought so . . . Or was that after . . .?" In deep contemplation, he continued, "Yes, yes . . . I suppose you're right . . .. But it was *after*, you know . . ."

"Yes, Bruce, yes. You're so close," I thought to myself, now only half-hopeless. What was it that Chesterton said, though, about hope? Oh, throw it all, Lord. He would remember. Ah!

> As long as matters are really hopeful, hope is a mere flattery or platitude; it is only when everything is hopeless that hope begins to be a strength at all. Like

all the Christian virtues, it is as unreasonable as it is indispensable.

That was it: *unreasonable* but *indispensable.*

"Ahh, after what I don't remember. But *He* was different, I know, I think. Had to be . . . Never mind that now. Are you hungry?" he asked.

"Yes, dear. Of course." I sighed.

"There's that *dear*, again. What is with this woman? Can't say I mind hearing it, though, I suppose. Sounds nice, from her lips anyway," I heard him mutter under his breath.

"What'll it be?"

"Chocolate croissants, and maybe some ice cream, and then I really must be going."

I sensed the heaviness setting in again, so at odds with the light and airy way in which he should carry himself, though his appetite seemed in-tact, in portion and in preference. Still, the shroud of that old burden had set its mast against him indeed, against that airy way again.

"Yes, it is that time, isn't it," I relinquished, wrapping my arm through his, pulling him close one last time as the rain began to fall. "*Unreasonable as it is indispensable*," as it were.

IV

The Cape

BRUCE, AND HER

ANOTHER GRUELING FLIGHT, ANOTHER tired mission. The sense that man was not meant to fly always came over me, on any flight, really, whether short or long. Though the suspicion grew wildest at or around the fifth hour of these legs. We were all Icarus's at that time. It seemed I always tried to sleep and always tried not to wake at that hour too, thinking how long I had been here, trapped in this canister, with such small windows and such thick, old air, and that incessant drone of the engines over the wings. Surely, we were soon to land.

It would be the eleventh hour before that reality on this journey, however. The bell tolled as the captain's voice over the intercom announced we were preparing to land. "At last," I thought. Before the fasten seat belt sign ignited, I decided that I should stand and walk a bit, for fear of going mad with that confined feeling.

I stood, turned to my right, set a slow pace, discreetly stretching alive joints and muscles and tendons in my legs, and saw her. Our eyes met as she stowed a book in her handbag. She half-smiled as she tucked her hair behind her left ear. Such beautiful eyes and such bright, blonde hair, almost white in that pale anywhere else unflattering LED light. She stood also, just as I was approaching her row, a middle row, again to my right. I stopped beside her, motioning and nodding for her to step out in front of me. She smiled and said, "Thanks. And, hello."

"Hello there," I replied. "Were you getting restless, too?"

"Oh, yes. Too much time sitting, too much time pretending you're not on a metal tube in the sky, going somewhere so fast with the feeling of nowhere to go."

I smiled and nodded in agreement. "Too true, too true."

As she walked, just in front of me, I could tell she kept her pace subdued, and she stood a little to my left, open, so as to make herself accessible, to conversation, I thought, glancing back every other step or so, adding to the appeal. I noticed she was thin but not frail—athletic—as tall as me but not intimidating—average—fair-skinned but not freckled—smooth—smartly dressed but not vogue—modern—vain moving but not prideful, for vanity by its nature was at least concerned with the thoughts of others, I remembered, and not merely concerned with self and its reflection—confident. She spoke with a faint accent, Russian or Baltic, I presumed. Her hair was so long and so straight that it nearly touched her waist.

As we neared the rear of the cabin, she turned and faced me, looking straight in my eyes. I spoke first, "I'm Bruce, by the way."

"Anna," she answered.

"Pleasure," I replied, and offered my hand to hers. I turned and ushered her in front of me again, and inquired, "What were you reading?"

"Oh, just Orwell's *1984*."

"Ah, the dystopia."

She snickered, "Indeed."

"'The best books . . . tell you what you know already,' don't they? But then, that year really wasn't as bad as they thought, now was it?"

"I wouldn't know. I'm a '90's chick, as they say," quoting the euphemism in obvious but playful mockery of the American vernacular.

"'90's," I thought. "How young?" We reached her seat. "Well, it was very nice meeting you, Anna. Perhaps I'll see you around town?"

"I think you will," she answered, with the certainty of all women who have made up their mind, made a plan in that mind, and made a determination in their hearts to carry it through. I was content to climb up and into that web her mind was in that very moment weaving. Who knew how long it would spin, how wide it would spread? We stopped in the aisle by her row again, awkwardly, I thought later.

"Where are you staying?" she continued.

"At a house on the coast, outside the city, beyond the naval station and the harbor."

"Oh, me too!" she exclaimed. "Well, not in that same house, of course, but in a B&B in town, just across the wall from the base. Why don't you come into town tomorrow morning and we'll have a coffee, ya?"

"Capital!" I almost shouted, startling an old woman in the exit row to my right. Calming down, "I'll be in at ten."

"Good," she said, pulling pen from pocket—from my jacket pocket—writing her name and her handle on a napkin stained with lipstick and smelling of Clair De Lune. "Clear moon," I reflected, what I once knew as a lesser light and a suite or a score I always knew by ear but never by name, what she probably only knew as a parfum. Or was it only a perfume? At least it was a classier scent, though not my favorite. Curious just how it masked cigarettes and, was it? Yes, vodka. "Surprising," I thought.

I snapped to, realizing fully now how awkward we were together, standing in the aisle, especially upon discovery that the vague rabble over the intercom was the pilot's final approach beacon, and at seeing a rather panicked looking face standing behind Anna's, wanting very much to find his seat. The nose was down.

"See you in the morning?"

"Yes," she said. "Till then, goodbye."

"Goodbye," I returned cheerfully, with another nod, almost bowing this time. "'Till then.' How clever, how quaint."

I smiled as I sat, fastened my seat belt, and day-dreamt of morning. As the plane descended, though, I fell under that strange suspicion that I was being watched. Perhaps Anna set her gaze to me, having the same mind to dream of morning and where we would wander, together.

◆ ◆ ◆

23

MORNING, AND THE WATCHWOMAN

"Where are you now, in the story, I mean?" I asked her, breathing heavily, having just sat down from my more-brisk-than-perhaps-necessary walk into town; the sea air still on my clothes, those odd little birds about the beach still on my mind, the sun flickering in through the open windows behind our table set for two just inside the second story balcony.

"A quote about the past, I think. I read it just now, while I was waiting, not long of course, waiting for you, I mean," she replied, thumbing through the well-worn pages, eagerly, I noticed. "Here, just here, ya . . .

'Who controls the past controls the future. Who controls the present controls the past.'"

"Hmm, why yes, perhaps. But the past, 'The past is like a foreign country; they do things differently there.'"

"Oooo, I like that, very much. Who said it?"

"I don't remember," I breathed out with a little laugh and a cough. "I must have been *very* far abroad when I first read it." She chuckled too, rolled her eyes, and turned up her nose as she turned up her glass. In time, in the short time we spoke, we moved to and from the topics of the day, the people in our world, and the stories we'd heard, all throughout together musing at how clever words and we could be, and I thought hers, the perfect mind for me. There was that sense again, though, like the eyes of the world had fallen on my collar, or at least two more eyes than normal. I turned over my shoulder, trying unassumingly to find the watching one. "Huh," I thought after scanning the room to no avail. "A phantom sense, then."

"Will you excuse me?" Anna asked as she stood, downing the last ounce of her glass.

"What's that?" coming to. "Oh, yes, of course," I acknowledged, half-standing for courtesy. Sitting back down, I watched her make her way to the lavatory. Next moment, there was some commotion to my left and I saw a stately woman move swiftly from her table, rattling the dishes as she rushed off. She followed Anna in. "Was it who I thought it was? Yes, I think so . . . Hartley, L.P. Hartley," I remembered, turning back, reaching across the table, thumbing a corner of that old book. The pages were soft, the sound soothing. *"The past . . . like a foreign country."*

It was a long time waiting for Anna. "Was that her name?" That light from the window was so bright now. The sun must be on the rise, high on the horizon. "What was I saying before she left? Had we even ordered?" The clouds rolled over the sun. A server approached the table, saying something about the woman. "Or did she say *women*?" She stood for a second or an hour, it seemed anyway, I couldn't recall. I only remembered the note she set on the table, folded in squares, the first word alone visible; the wet, black ink and the room growing dark.

Time—what the parchment read.

I slipped the note into the middle of *1984*, tucked the tattered book under my arm, and set off, down and out of that tavern, restaurant, room, back to my hotel, hermitage, house, whatever quarter on the coast I had found this round. Down, down, down the lane. Cars on the curves, canon fire in the Cape, an east wind on my collar, tempest at Table, and those damnable birds waddling on the beach, squawking and mocking all my way home. "No balm here," I thought as my pace quickened. "Pursuer at my neck. Worn out, no rest. Conflicts without, fears within. Turmoil comes, time flees. Would that it were evening!"

◆ ◆ ◆

THE END OF THE WORLD

"Now son, the woman is speaking again," the old man started.

I nodded in acknowledgement, and in approval once more . . .

I followed Bruce home that night. I knew the housekeeper there at the too-yellow taupe mansion on the rocks. We, eh, *I* had been there enough by now. I stayed in his quarters in these times, which were separate from the main house, but still connected by the cobblestone driveway. Percival was his name, or "Percy" as he liked, and he, if you are curious, stayed down the street at the B&B when I was in. Only a boy by my judgment, of the surfer sort, tan

25

and ruddy with tussled blonde hair and a dazed but happy look to him. He kept the house well, and he was, when you needed him, always in earshot, even down the street. "Ruddy but reliable," he would say of him.

I watched Bruce through the window, standing outside in the night mist, so thick and so cold that it felt like rain, but it never seemed to rain in this country. "The skies have withheld the dew," I thought. Having foregone Percy's cloak, which still hung by the quarter door, I shivered a bit, clasping my arms. No moon tonight, no stars. I watched Bruce saunter out of the stone shower cut out of the wall, moving slowly into the living area, towel on waste and nothing other. He sat in the dimness of that house, no room or nook ever very well lit, save for those little coffers on the walls which housed the oddly painted African masks, each having their own accent. I saw him notice the book on the table before him, where he'd first set it an hour ago, beside his trademark copy of *Tradecraft*. He drew it up, thumbed the pages, found the note, opened it, and read my words:

> *My Dear Bruce,*
>
> *Anna, the woman you met on the plane, she wasn't right for you; she isn't best for you. None of them are, and I told her as much in that peculiarly well-kempt restaurant toilet. I told her about you, about your past, about you and I and where we'd wandered these last three years, about the light and the shadows, the dust and the dawn, the waking and the dreaming. I told her about us, Bruce . . .*
>
> *Know that I will always be here, beside you as often as I can, behind you the rest of the way, watching, waiting, wading back in each night, each day, until that day dawns, and God knows it will, that hour, that moment, that instant when you awake, when you come to, to me.*
>
> *Isn't it time, Bruce?*
>
> *Captain, my Captain, come home.*
>
> *Yours,*
> *Ruthie*
>
> *P.S. We aren't the type to "steal rolls." Remember that.*

26

He looked up for a moment, pondering, then he turned ever-so-slightly round toward the window, looking as if he knew there were someone there. Then, alas, he turned up his brows, nodded his head as if he'd had a merely quaint and passing thought, and then he retired to his room. I turned from the window and listed back to Percy's quarters, through the mist.

Morning would come again, though, and I would take him by storm—"pale lightning and peals of thunder, flashing and crashing and shaking cruel thrones and dry bones"—he'll reap the whirlwind of . . . Oh, dear, he would've said something like that, in a lecture. My, how he talked when he taught. "He will see tomorrow. Yes, tomorrow. He'll come to. It was high time he did."

At the quarter door, I reached within the key box high and right of the frame, and discovered something inside I hadn't noticed on the way in. It was a note, crumpled and damp from the mist. I unraveled it:

> *Mum,*
> *Surely this time, love. Hold on hope, as he'd schooled me and shown you. Ring if ya need nething.*
>
> *Cheers,*
> *Percy*

For a moment, I was nearly overcome with emotion. "What a sweet boy," I said under my breath, wiping my nose, turning the key. "Tomorrow, then, to the Cape and Good Hope."

♦ ♦ ♦

Before dawn's light, I stood affront the only full-length mirror on the property, toes down, knee bent, fastening straps, draping silk, ruffling lacy bits, tying and untying knots, turning to-and-fro, aft and forward, looking and seeing, putting on and taking off. The whole gambit I packed and nothing came forth or came on appealing enough, I thought, so I went with a summer suit, bright and boyish shorts, and a solid white top, covered partly with a camisole, then a ruffled, sheer, and off-the-shoulder cover-up—"That's the one"—and a wide-brimmed hat, and big, dark shades, though all would find their way into my tote before I met him. All but the suit and cover-up—covering less now than ever—made their way with me as I crept through the arched entrance and into the room where he lay. I resisted the desire—with some effort—to crawl into bed with him as I slinked by, biting my lip, then turning and taking my place by the windows—floor-to-ceiling—as the sun rose over the mountains, pale orange then purple in streaks through the mist, spreading out over the water and breaking in through the house.

I waited with no sweat or shivers, fears or nerves, but in a new mood now, with a new hope, and a new strength mingled with what remained of an old and indistinguishable excitement. I watched the beams creep too now, over the floor, up onto the bed and duvet where he lay, alighting on his face, which twitched and frowned as he awoke with a sigh. I turned—only slightly—letting the breeze from the one open window ease the cover-up fully off my shoulders and onto my elbows. Catching it, tossing my hair—toes down, knee up, tightening what I could—I met his eyes, stared only for an instant, and said what he wanted,

"Good morning, Captain . . ."

Bruce blinked twice, braced up on one elbow, and looked at me in a sober confusion.

"Had I lost my appeal?" I thought, feeling that recurring insecurity welling up within. But he came to, and came to me. He was an opportunist after all—all men were—and I exhaled. All was well that morning, but the day had only just begun.

We tarried in the house for a while, then on the patio, on the porch, on the lawn out back where we could see clearly now the end of Table Mountain off in the distance. At that moment, I remembered the thickness of the mists up there, rolling through the courtyards, chilling to the bone, blowing so swiftly over that flat peak that you understood why the guides liken the long view of the whole scene to a cloth falling off a table. It certainly looked that way from this distance. But on the plateau, with the mists of that mountain rushing over and around and even through you, the experience was more like that of a magician who tore at the cloth from somewhere beyond the world, snatching it so violently and so relentlessly that you felt as if you were the crystal wears and fine settings, shaking and rattling and teetering atop the mountain table, without yield.

"Let's go for a drive. What do you say, Jack?"

"Well, I say, what are we driving, then? And to where?" he chimed in, almost automatically.

"Oh, I have a place in mind. And we'll take my car. It's in the garage." He'd fallen under my spell by now. He was in that state where wanderlust—or perhaps, lust alone—outweighed sense and sensibility, where silly questions faded and everything fell away after *What?* and *Where?*, coming into *Alright's*, and *Very well's*, and *That sounds lovely's*. But such ignorant infatuation came at a price, for time always began to allude him here on this precipice, where he knew no other but the present. Another trip might rouse him, though, and I was so wanting to see the park at the end of the world, those heights at the southern-most tip of that realm.

We packed my tote, he helped me stow the top, and we roared out of the garage, down the cobbled driveway, into the street to make our way round the coast in that white Jaguar he once spied from the tarmac on our first visit. On our way out of the naval town, I pointed out the venders on the street, suggesting we might pay them a visit on the way in. I always liked to look, you know, and sometimes support the local economies, but really, just to look and to mouth with the natives. But Bruce only scoffed and muddled under his breath, "Same old junk, in every city, in every country."

◆ ◆ ◆

On the spirited, winding drive within that open-top, joy-of-a-Jaguar, we headed down the coast toward a place where it was rumored you stood so high and could see so far over the southern world, that if you squinted hard enough, you might see the frozen shores of Antarctica. We stopped a time or two along that coastal road, to gaze over the cliffs, once finding a pod of whales in the surf below, rising and falling, blowing and rolling, in the shallows, I thought. But Bruce said the water was much too dark to have it less than four or five fathoms deep. We hoped we'd catch them breach, but they must have been some other kind of whale. We drove again, through mountain passes, toward sharp and blind corners, around soaring walls and jagged cliffs, the African sun beating down—*South* African sun, that is—beaming all through that crisp, dry air, warming it with hints of sea and salt and desert-edge rock.

We stopped for lunch in a small town that almost looked Italian in age and architecture, eating out instead of on the picnic we'd packed in my tote. At table, I told him of a time I'd met an old woman in an even smaller town on the other side of the Cape, a place with only a single café on the rocks. It was a bed & breakfast wedged between some raucous waves and an estuary where the sea fed a river behind the town, a river which slowed into an otherworldly-still, seemingly Amazonian jungle scape with two steep green hills on either side of a long, crescent beach, hills that, as you walked along the rim of that blunt peninsula, just around the corner of a boardwalk bridge, would tower up over you as you stood on the soft, cool sand, feeling very small and very calm, and very much in awe. East London was that other world.

The woman I sat with at otherworld café, told me of a time when her and her late husband first visited the park to where we were presently en route. They, the woman and her husband, of course, had heard of baboons that roam wild in the brush there. Visitors to the park were warned not to feed them, for the monkeys might become aggressive, as selfish and as simple-minded as they are, you know. The husband, knowing what he did from his family's business, much appreciated how baboons were terrified of snakes. Having planned their ruse, the couple entered the park to wait at an opening in the brush where they arrested their car. The husband placed a toy snake in a brown paper bag, coiled it, ruffled up the mouth of the bag, and the wife tossed some bread crumbles out of the car. Then they together awaited their prey.

In a moment, a mother baboon rushed out of the bushes, baby on her belly. The monkey noticed the bread, stopped, and sat on her haunches, soon mashing and fingering the pieces into her mouth, paying little attention to our couple in the car nearby. The husband, spying the right moment, crinkled up the bag and tossed it out the window toward the mother monkey. Looking up suddenly from her bread meal, the monkey caught sight of the projectile, and being accustomed to treats distributed in that manner, she bundled over to the bag, set her baby down, and began tearing into it. When the monkey saw the snake, she jumped back, then fainted!

The couple laughed and laughed and then, when the monkey came to, they watched her bundle—slower now—back to the bag and baby. The baboon caught one glimpse of the snake again, and fainted once more! The couple were in tears together, and their day was made. And as the wife remembered the moment, reflecting at the small café table as the sound of sea waves billowed over the soft clinks of dishes faintly audible behind the counter, she said of her husband, "Sweet, sweet liar, he was," recalling to mind his mirth, it seemed, and at the same time, some terror and a tragedy trying to run in and around and ruin her happy thought. A tear welled in her eye, but then the wife smiled, as any widow might who had made her peace with the memory of him. "Sweet, Sweet, liar, you know, dear. That he was. And such a *pleasure* . . .," trailing off her words into the past. I found out later that the family still owned the safari land in the south, *all* the safari land, and had made a game preserve with giraffes, elephants, lions, and cheetahs you could pet. I discovered the truth of the tragedy also, but that is perhaps a story better reserved for another time.

"What a life," Bruce said, breaking in. "They must be wealthy."

"Quite so, in more ways than monetary, dear."

In an hour or so, back on the road, we passed one, a baboon, that is, just outside the park, sitting in the middle of the street, chewing away at something without care of the world around it. We stopped at the gates, paid our entry, parked, and set off for that last cliff at the southern-most-tip of that world.

◆ ◆ ◆

It was hotter now, but the air, still crisp off the water and still dry, every now and again, caught our hair in gusts and squalls, then calmed to breezes by the time we made it to the base of the stairs, where the wind ushered us upward onto that corridor of cliffs which led to the most delightful lookout area, a place up and beyond the too-oft visited lighthouse. Bruce noticed the warning signs on either side and, glancing up, picked out the resting benches marked out at very close intervals, he thought, up on left and on right, every

31

twenty or thirty steps between the thin log handrails which were set up along the edges of the stairway, hand rails that were, oddly enough, not continuous, leaving short gaps of rail-less, unleveled, rocky-stepped walkway. Bruce chuckled as he read the small green sign to me: *Please take care while using the stairs.*

"It rhymes, well sort of."

"Come along, dear. The view awaits us," I beckoned, noticing again the desert trees and shrubs, the fine sand, the yellow and tan rocks protruding everywhere out of the ground, and the wonderful contrast of the ocean, which seemed to mount an assault from every direction, wanting to close in the coast from below in blues and greens and white-capped sea foam waves.

We made our way up the steps that were, in fact, quite steep, I in front, for I remembered the way, what was always a suspect and wearisome and impossible to discern direction for Bruce, who by now was a step or two behind me. I glanced back over my left shoulder every now and again, to smile at him. Passing the white lighthouse, ten, twenty, thirty steps up from its base, we climbed and climbed until we reached a turret, a piece of ruined history it always seemed to me, only a quarter high of what it once was, with an open roof and a stone wall stacked only waist-high, which you could stand before and feel safe looking down over, down into that blue and green sea assailing the coast by dragoons of white swells hundreds and hundreds of feet below you.

I turned back once more to Bruce to ensure he was content to stop at the turret lookout for a rest and a short view, when I saw him slip. Time slipped too, ebbing and drawing with the surf and the sieging sounds below as he stumbled sharply forward, stopped short, stared up at me, then fell back.

"Bruuuce!" I started in horror, gasping as my breath ran out for fear. I could only watch him fall as one hand reached toward him, and the other covered my mouth as I gasped again. Like a still frame film, frame after frame, a new fright at every slide, pausing and playing, still then in motion, I saw his back flat against the stairs on the first tumble, dust kicking up from the dry and rocky steps— another slide—then his whole body flipped over at the head— slide—sideways now, left toward the edge of the stairs—slide—then

CRACK! went his hip on the open end of that thin but solid log of a handrail. The impact spun him round to where he landed feet-out and head towards me, on his bottom. He bounced there on three or four steps before he arrested ten or fifteen feet beneath me. "*God*," I thought. "Thank heavens he didn't tumble all the way down."

I rushed to him, found him still on his back, hearing soft and terrible groans from his lips, then gasps and gurgles, then silence and an eerie quiet all-round. That moment, by his side, was perhaps the only time my prized line would be impeccably untimely, and it was, the whole scene, that is, for a long while, the only time I would want him to forget. For if he remembered, he would never let me live that line down.

We never made it to our lookout, nor to the sign of Good Hope at the end of the world, nor did we make it anywhere else in the park, except to the medical tent, and then onto and inside the ambulance for Bruce. We left that place early in the afternoon. I drove the Jaguar again, trailing behind the medical transport, thinking and praying and worrying all back through the cliff-side curves. I had heard that after our visit, the sign beside those park stairs grew three sizes, and changed a shade of yellow and red. "Here's the hospital, at last."

The doctors made quick work of Bruce. Diagnosis? A deep bruise and a crack on the hip's bone, but nothing sinister or irrecoverable, so we were told. Though the doctor did say Bruce may, for the rest of his days, walk with a limp, and that he may need a cane in time. We left the hospital as the sun was setting; top still down, to make room for the crutches.

What a loathsome drive it was. And there were no churches on the drive back to the too-yellow or too-taupe house, I noticed. Someone told us, when asked, that they were hidden in neighborhoods, and of one in a village far, far away, guarded by night by men with machine guns. I remembered how we once visited a church like that, only a few miles from the otherworld café. The old church buildings we would see in the cities were apartments now, she said, or discos, and no longer places to pray.

"Who are you?" Bruce said abruptly at a stoplight, eyeing me warily over the crutches.

I sighed. "Ruthie, my name is Ruthie, and I'm just here to take you home."

"Oh. 'Ruthie.' What a sweet name," I heard him murmur under his breath, in a new but old air of oblivion, but at least it was a peaceful bliss.

I pulled off the side of the road at the street vendors we first glimpsed on our way out. Snickers could be heard from passersby, who noticed Bruce's newly-prescribed crutches showing still so high out of the tiny convertible. "Like there were space for them anywhere other."

"Stay in the car, will you? Rest that old hip," I said to him, stepping out and shutting the car door.

In the make-shift road-side market, I sought something regal for Bruce, regal *and* useful, perhaps. Browsing through the cheap jewelry works and colorful clay sculpting's, I came upon a barrel filled to the brim with all sizes of intricately carved canes, of mahogany, I thought, and so thickly lacquered that you could almost make out your reflection in them. Beside the canes, on a low table, set out on a blue cloth, there were, laid out like a miniature menagerie, all kinds of animal heads—elephants, crocodiles, wolves, horses and ducks, dogs and serpents, in silver, bronze, and gold—but I thought the golden eagle the most elegant, the most regal, and the most American, something a true American scholar would wield. I paid the man for the regal head and its mahogany neck in what currency I had left, and made away out to Bruce and the Jag. "Oh!" I thought as I approached the car. "A purple ribbon would have made a nice touch. Ah, well. Never mind that now."

Back inside the quaint little town, we pulled into the harbor lot to dine at the finest restaurant in the Cape, one with a patio overlooking the inlet. The naval ships were all at their posts, on display, for it was Fleet Week. The destroyers had just begun their evening show. The biggest and loudest of the cannons fired all through our dinner, their tracer rounds lighting the sky in flashes of yellow and green, streaking through the night like glittered stars shot from deep earth to deep heaven. Bruce leaned back, looked out over the scene with a twinkle in his eye that shot across the table with an imagined nostalgia, and said, "I could eat forever at the sound of the articles of war."

"It gets old, dear. It really does," I suggested with fatigue, but also with warmth.

Next morning, we awoke in the yellow house together. I dressed and readied and planned our way to the airport, where he'd asked me to drive him. I left the crutches in the closet, packed all our things in what trunk there was, and set his new cane between the seats. He emerged from the bedroom, ready as well, and we were in the Jag and off again.

On our way, we passed that odd little beach which was home to those odd little birds, as he'd called them on occasion. The sight of it, of a couple laying side by side, flat on their backs on a big, black rock in the surf surrounded by penguins, noiseless and as silly looking as you might imagine, some wading in and waddling out of that shallow surf, but most, burrowed in the sand on their bellies, was almost too perfect to forget.

"Wait, wait, wait," I cut in. "There were penguins . . . *on the beach?*"

"Why, yes, my boy. They are warm weather waddlers," the old man came back. "Now . . . where— . . ."

"The little beach. She was driving by the little beach, with the penguins."

"Ah, yes, of course . . ."

We drove around that corner, over the mountain pass, out into the warm light of morning, and on to the next, then the last destination, if all came to pass, as it were.

35

V

Atlanta

BRUCE AND THE BLUFF

RATTLES AND SHAKES, RAILS and screeches, graffiti and the overhead call, down under then up over ground again, the hard bench and the scarred window, stop after stop, this and the rest on the long ride to the end of the line. I had, today, an appointment at eight a.m. in Suwanee, a residential realm quite far from the airport, and far enough from the city. My ride was to arrive at a quarter 'til eight. It was seven thirty as I glanced up at the lighted map of the line, which revealed seven solid dots to my destination.

Remembering now, again, how to panic well, I sat up in that stern seat and looked around me. What I saw was what anyone might see on any old subway car: an elderly woman in an apron and a work get-up, much like an antiquated cleaning uniform, some youths huddled in groups, standing and staring at their phones, every one of them with their ears plugged, and an aged and rugged, scruffy and homeless looking man with feet bare, face bearded, and head covered with a Vietnam War cap. That man was staring at me as I glanced up at him. I quickly looked away, back at the youths, out the window, then around at the man again in a moment, casually and cautiously, finding his gaze still fixed on me. With a wild and crazed eye, the man stared without end, at me—through me, it seemed. Just when I felt I couldn't bear it any longer, the man stormed at me, and in two long and forceful steps he was before me.

"Yerrr lost!" the crazed man declared, clapping his hands on his knees, stooping at his waist to address me eye to eye.

"I say, whatever do you mean, sir?" I said pompously, with an accent retrieved from my previous destinations, no doubt, and in that peculiar tone any man accused might take instinctively, innocent or not, without thought to the charge.

"I said, 'You're *lost!*'" the man repeated, but louder and in a less distinctly Scottish accent now, with some saliva and a stronger emphasis on "lost." "I've seen it before, in a newsboy at the edge of Khe Sanh, who saw with his peepers what no boy should see. I said to him, 'Go home, *boy*. You're lost! You don't belong. This ain't a place fer paper-*boys*. It's a place fer killers, fer soldiers, fer the dead and the damned!'"

I shuddered, stunned. Wide-eyed and fumbling, attempting to formulate a rebuttal to no avail, I tried still to speak, accent in all. "I-I, say," but the man cut in.

"It's in yer eyes, boy. You ain't a soldier. Now go home! *Go home*," he finished. But still he stood staring, hunched over, right before me, for what seemed like an hour. The train eased to a stop and the man finally stood, demanded two dollars from my wallet, walked deliberately out the now open doors, and he was gone.

"My *God*," I thought. "What a demented man," returning my wallet to its rightful place. "And what did he mean 'I'm no soldier.' Tuh, the *nerve*." Even so, a mass of discomfort hardened within me, and I felt wounded and cold and heavy, even a little ashamed, indeed like a boy, a boy who had just sat at the receiving end of a schoolmaster's reprimand, or even a child at the chastisement of his mother. I looked up at the lighted map once more. Three dots.

When the train eased to a stop again at my station, I exited to stand on the platform which overlooked the parking lot. It was eight a.m. and I saw no car and no friend. I stood on that wood-planked platform till eight thirty. Now eight forty-five. By nine, perhaps for the first time again, by sense or by what seemed a recurring and a waking dream, I started to see how this well was dry. Perhaps no appointment awaited me, no friend or car, meeting or mission;

no person or place, here or anywhere, waited for this one silly boy without any real charge. "Wells without water, clouds carried with a tempest; to whom the mist of darkness is reserved for ever." Is this what the prophets meant, said so long ago to a people prone to wander? To what was *I* returning, day-in and day-out, a dog or a sow, over and again, to vomit or to wallow in the mud, I could not remember, for the mist.

I stepped off that planked platform, then back in and onto that rambling wreck of a Georgia train. The wheels whined and rolled up to speed as I dazed, looking out into the distance, over the city and up at the clouds rolling in, through the battle-hardened window, upon the hard-bottom bench, dozing off toward sleep. When I came to, without a glance at lights or dots, I rushed off the train and onto a low and dark place, a cold and damp platform, metal-grated with grimy, black steps leading up and out and all around. I was underground.

The people, what few there were on the underground station, cut suspicious looks at me. In a corner by a large fan, a group of eyes watched me as I walked, backs all turned, with shifty necks over shoulders and shuffles of feet mixed with murmurs and what sounded like cruel jeers. "I better get to the surface," I thought, adding a jump to my step. I found the stairway up and out, made my way through it, and breached that surface, but not into the light of day I expected. The world I rose up into was an uncanny, an uneasy, an unsettling street, on which every fiber and every nerve rose up within me to make it known to my mind that I was in danger. I might try and describe it to you.

A haze hung about that place; a shadow and a thicker mist lingered there. It felt like an oppressive force was closing in from all sides, like the whole town was in its clutches, like there were very real "Invisible Enemies" all round: on the sidewalk beside me, by the corner store, behind the shirtless man running down the alley across the street; enemies all the same, ones who treated nations and generations like merchandise; silent killers in the streets, acting above ground—moving, scheming, stealing out in the open air now, destabilizing and disabling and disenfranchising, oppressing the whole of the population here and around this world. Like black moons and black mornings, dark forces, devastation and despair.

But the sense of it I'd never felt anywhere else in the world, not like that, and that sense had nothing to do with the mere look of the place: the obvious socio-economic strain and the accompanying signs, the food deserts, wastelands, the subsidization and gentri-fication—all distractions, I thought, though the sights of war for certain, but mere symptoms in all societies, only expressions of an oppression that had everything to do with the galactic polity of the real "Princes of Persia," those "powers and principalities," the whis-pers behind kings' decrees, and what really were, especially in the child's still opened mind, the real culprits behind every bump in the night. In essence, they were part and parcel to the diagnosis of our day, of any day or any age for that matter: the movers and shapers and blinders who fostered the banality of evil in and around the unaware, glorifying to men the mind of indifference, what was, I thought, the real root of all kinds of ordinary evil that seeded places like this into all kinds of extraordinary moral decay. It was The Great Bluff, and I was afraid, of all of it, for I could have sworn I heard, thick and long, just above me in that moment, the gradual rising and falling of wings, and felt the hot air of some whisperer too close for any comfort.

I paused still, though, at how true it was, that before me at the top of that last grimy step lay the wages of war from another world's invaders. Cities rose and fell by their hands. This one, where I stood, had fallen, be it only a town in a city. So many lived in darkness there unbeknownst to them, as the darkness grew larger and louder at every hour. Such servants of subterfuge, of some adversary who now acted out in the broad but here dim daylight. And there was, I imagined in that moment, no one to stand against them, no one left in the gap, not here, or so I thought, thus I thought all the people purchased already, persuaded into a life of pleasure and paradox and final peril, forgetting altogether that brighter worlds on the surface fell from within by the same sword, or serpent, or simple but sinister deception. Had all worlds faced the same temptation?

I trembled at my thoughts on the edge of that Bluff, then hur-ried back underground, leaning on my cane at each step, fearing the feel of that place, wanting for the taste of something true or right or noble, or even something simply pure. I would settle for anything *good*. There must be some light somewhere, but not there, not in that place, not ever again, not for me, I decided. The train came down and I boarded. Out and up and away to another, lighter place, I hoped.

◆ ◆ ◆

TWO OR THREE VISITORS, AND A SPARROW'S WORTH

I saw no one memorable on the southbound journey to my hotel. North Avenue was the station I sought. Of course, I got off on the wrong side of the train and ended up at street level again, in an unfamiliar place. At least the air was clear here, and nothing uncanny lurked about. I had never seen this part of the city, though I was not in the least concerned. I found my marker in the skyline, the copper-tipped bank tower, and set off in that direction.

My surroundings became more familiar as I walked. Just ahead of me, I saw a man I knew, someone I had seen before, I was sure of it. Virgil was his name, and he was friend to someone important in this burrow, I thought, someone of significance to me and to all who wandered here. I decided to tail him.

Virgil kept a few yards ahead of me, carrying two white plastic grocery bags in his right hand, walking as if he was to make a delivery. I hung back to see where he was headed when we both came out into an open space beside a main MARTA station. It was North Avenue Station, indeed. A wave of the surreal came over me as I set a slow pace further out into the open, staying closest to the street, making my way toward the crosswalk. To my left I saw Virgil approach a huge man in a wheelchair. He was so large that I thought he could not stand at all, nor could he even move without that chair. Virgil handed the man on wheels one of the white bags. They looked busy in conversation soon thereafter, and what feelings that would have compelled me to speak with them, I ignored.

I faced the street and pressed the button on the pole that I knew would light the crosswalk. As I waited, the giant man in the chair kept wheeling through my mind, so I turned and waived at them, he and Virgil, but they must not have seen me. I faced the street again and just as I did so, a white cargo van turned on signal into the lane from across the opposite side of the road. As it passed over the crosswalk in front of me, it slowed, it's windows down, and I saw the driver as clear as day—short-haired, gray shirt, dark sunglasses—pointing over my left shoulder, staring dead at me. I was the only one on the sidewalk, at least in my field of view, so I assumed he was pointing at something—or someone—behind me. I turned slowly around to my left and saw . . .

"It was the woman, wasn't it!? I mean, it was Ruthie!" I gasped out.

"Quiet, boy! You'll spoil the story."

"Ughhh, okay, okay . . . Over your shoulder . . ."

It was the large man and Virgil again. I took this as a sign, from whence I did not know, but a sign nonetheless. I decided to venture over and chat with Virgil and the wheeled man.

As I approached the two men, they both greeted me with "Hello's," and I waived again as the big man wheeled toward me, leaving Virgil a little behind. He held out his hand and asked me how I was getting on. "It's hot!" I said bluntly, and I asked without thought if either of them needed anything.

The big man replied, "It *is* hot. I'm thirsty. Let's share a Cherry Ice."

"Where might I find one of those?" I asked.

"From the BP, two blocks that-a-way," he answered, pointing beyond the crosswalk, straight down North Avenue.

"Very well. You got it. One Cherry Ice." I asked Virgil from beyond if he wanted anything, but he only shook his head no.

I set off down the street, making my way toward the "BP." Two blocks walked, I crossed the street to the left, and reached my destination. As I neared the entrance, I greeted a man standing out front—casually, as any American man might, with no intent to conversation. "Hello," I said in a friendly way.

"How are *you* doing?" he asked forthright.

41

"I'm doing just fine, thank you . . . How are you?" I asked, in obligation, a little surprised at the forwardness and the seemingly legitimate interest in his question. He said he was well, but he moved toward me, placed his hand on my shoulder, and asked me for two dollars, or for exactly three dollars and forty-nine cents to buy a cup of coffee up the street. Remembering my tradecraft, I told him I hadn't any cash, but that I'd be happy to buy him something inside.

He stopped and stated unapologetically, "You look like a Christian."

"I am," I replied back, without thought again. I asked the man his name.

"Dion," he offered, shaking my hand. What he said next surprised me even more. Dion told me he had two Scriptures for me. The first was from Hebrews. He quoted as follows: "Do not forget to show hospitality to strangers, for thereby some have entertained angels unawares." And the second, from Matthew, he quoted also, in part, in paraphrase: "Are not the sparrows sold for a penny? So don't be afraid; you are worth more than many sparrows." All throughout and in between, the man seemed to exclaim uncontrollably, "God is so good! He provides just what we need, doesn't He?" as if Dion were the mouthpiece for some other speaker behind the man.

I stood there, in front of that corner gas station, astounded at the timely word, though I did not quite understand what made the word timely. I expressed to Dion how much those words meant to me, nonetheless, having just emerged from that abyss of a Bluff, and they were, the words, that is, perhaps, just what I needed to hear, though again, only so in that muddled confusion where mind did not well assign meaning to emotion. I asked him what he wanted from within, and what follows was his order: Coffee with two creams and three Equals, and an apple fritter. "Coming right up," I said, and headed inside.

In line, and the line was quite long with the morning rush, I assumed if Dion really wanted his coffee and donut, he would wait. And besides, I had nowhere else to go, save to return a Cherry Ice to that large man at the station. What was his name? Will, or Bob, or Earnest? That was his name, I do believe. What's more, if either departed from their places, I would thoroughly enjoy either order—or both.

I noticed a man waiting to the right of the counter. He smiled and nodded at me. I smiled and nodded back in kind, obliging again in that cordial manner most commonplace men share. He was wearing a uniform, with knee pads and a helmet clad with a small headlight, what I imagined was useful in a cave or a tunnel, perhaps. His shirt read "Atlanta Gas and Light."

The uniformed man spoke and asked how I was. I replied that I was well and mentioned that it looked as if he worked hard. He laughed and explained to me a little of what he did on the day to day, indeed underground, repairing cables beneath houses and businesses all over the city. Next, he asked of me the most common conversational question, and the most natural here, what I did for a living. Without hesitation, even carelessly, plainly, calmly I said, "I am a missionary, sir," though I must have looked very strange to the man after I said this, for I was, within, as astonished at hearing my own words as any man might be who had just then, after many years of one-sided or silent, quiet or conversation-less friendship, heard his own dog speak a reply, or even his donkey, who said anything at all. And I was quite sure that feeling shown without. Regardless, the working man's eyes grew wide as he replied,

"*Really?* Very cool, man, very cool." And he leaned in and continued softly, "And I bet your work is harder than mine."

"It just might be," I answered, confirming his wager as right and as true as I knew it to be.

Then, he shook my hand, asked my name, and said, "God bless you, my friend," and walked off to work, I presumed.

By this time, it was my turn to order. I stepped to the counter and stated Dion's oddly specific beverage order, bought the last apple fritter, scooped up the coffee when it was ready, and headed back outside. He was waiting patiently just where I left him. I handed him the coffee and fritter and he thanked me with another blessing: "God bless you," and asked, "Did you get everything you need?"

"Yes, sir. I think I have everything I need," a little perplexed at his question. I nodded, smiled, and turned back inside for the wheeled man's Cherry Ice, which of course, I waited to purchase, for fear it might melt too soon in the summer city heat. The entire Ice transaction only consumed perhaps two minutes of time, for the line was much shorter at the center register, and when I walked back outside again, Dion was gone. Just gone. Not around the corner—as I checked—not down the street—as I looked—not in a car, nor on a bus, not anywhere to be found. Just gone, out of sight. I thought for a moment about what he had said to me. Chills came over me. I paused, then pressed on, Ice in hand, back to deliver the cherry treat.

When I reached the MARTA station, at the corner, Virgil and the wheeled man were posted where I left them, but another man had joined them, a thin, small, and shadowy looking man, but with bright eyes, whom I had never seen before. Approaching the three, I handed the big man his drink, assuring him it was all his, for we needn't share. He thanked me, slurped a huge gulp, wiped the sweat from his brow with a sigh, and the other men closed in around me. "Let's pray," said the large man. We all took shoulders. "Our Father, who art in heaven . . .," the small man began, in a voice as big as the sea, reciting the entire prayer, then after, beckoning, pleading, interceding for us all, that we would be men of that sort who might be counted among the strong and the righteous. He finished his prayer. I paused again, then spoke,

"I haven't said or heard a prayer like that in a long time. I thank you." They returned the sentiment, especially the man from the chair, as he slurped the last sip of his Ice. At this, I turned and walked, to where, I did not know, overwhelmed.

◆ ◆ ◆

MARQUIS HEIGHTS, THE WOMAN

I found him again nearing the crosswalk, thankful that I wasn't too late. A little out of breath from running down the street, thanks to a late train and a traffic jam, I stood on the third arm of the four-way intersection, awaiting my signal. I collected myself with a long and a deep breath, closed then opened my eyes, and breathed out a short prayer. White went the little lighted man to cross and walk, and I hurried across the street, North Avenue Station to my right, the college to my left. I made the street, cut left at the sight of Earnest and his gang, and I was upon him. My pace slowed again, taking in one last deep breath, easing out one last sigh, and ready was I as Bruce pressed in that silly shiny button on the big and black pole, which offered its shade to the street and not to us, as the sun rose higher out over the eastern sky behind us.

The light flashed. I strolled up just on his left and cupped his arm above the elbow. "Hey there. Don't I know you?" I asked coyly as Bruce turned toward me, calm again in his gaze, and half-smiling in that way he assumed when something that, to any other mind would be a world-shattering revelation, was for him only an instance that just arrived and then alighted, upon seeing my face. How that fleeting expression pained me.

"I-I don't think so," he replied, not stopping through the cross-walk, looking back at me in candid contemplation, then back ahead in kind insensibility, a familiar to me cycle which continued until we reached the road's end. Atop the sidewalk now, he stopped and addressed me again, "I'm Bruce, though. How might you know me? Or, eh, how might I know you?"

"Oh, I don't know. Have you ever made it as far as London?"

"A time or two, I think, but I don't remember much of the journey."

That was as true a statement as was ever uttered. "Well, I know I know you, but I just can't place it. I'm Ruthie," extending my hand.

"Bruce," he offered again with a shake and cordial smile.

"Where you headed?" I asked as he pivoted, and we together began walking side by side, westward again.

"I'm not sure, actually. How about you?"

"Some place *grand*. Have you ever been to The Marquis?"

"I don't really know. It sounds awfully familiar."

"Of course, it does," I thought to myself. "Care to join me?" I asked aloud, easing my hair behind my ear, trying very much to remember and so convey what it was like just learning to flirt. He paused for a few seconds, appearing to weigh some meaningful balance now in contemplation of exactly what terms I never quite discovered.

"I think I will. Lead the way, Ruth, is it?" meeting my brows and quarter tilt of the head. "Ruthie, I mean."

"That it is," nodding, brows down and relaxing. "And it's this way, straight ahead, and then we'll veer a little left through the college."

"Capital!" he bellowed in a familiar fondness of voice that signaled what I thought might be a breaking in and a coming to. Though I always seemed to feel this way here, nearing our journey's end, in what was a perpetual, no, a revolving state of my own hope or, my own denial. Hope it is, then, in the dream of time returning. Would that it might be true. It was, and it would be, soon now, time again. The open gate through the courtyard gardens of that otherwise always bricked and barred North Avenue church on our right, just now, was all the confirmation I needed in that moment, for as we passed by the cast iron door swung wide as it was, welcoming in all who would wander there, I felt, without question, some presence—thunderous but calming, in constant motion but immovable, wild but good, uncanny but familiar, colossal but near—the world itself I felt in that garden, and I smiled in awe, looking down and away to capture the encounter in memory, then carried on.

We crossed another walk into the college grounds, another left, cross and walk, through the dorm rows, down past the shelters, the museum, the factory and the aquarium, stopping again to cross and wait, the five rings and another park behind us where it looked as if they were filming a movie, or perhaps a commercial. The camera followed three couples in formal wear walking in procession, two-by-two and arm-in-arm with some distance between each pair, but all with joyous smiles on faces, thinking of what and heading to where I did not know, but I was certain by their appearance that their instruction was to be and to look and to walk and talk as if they together were full of hope, as if, perhaps, they had all come out from a marvelous ball celebrating someone or something or some great end. No queen to see here, though, but another eye, one with a sky view, what we faced as we awaited the little walk man.

We spoke very little on that side street journey, even at stops and intervals where we stood surrounded by city goers, travelers, vagabonds, business men and working women. In those moments, the quiet times, in the absence of small talk and what cheap banter I had yet to master, I felt we drew closer at every step, at every stop, at every closed-lip conversation. It was, you know, the person to whom you needn't speak all the time, even to or with at all when together, that was the person most right for you, and I had grown more and more sure of it then. Bruce would certainly agree, with an only slightly off-applied paraphrase, no doubt: "In so many words, you might say the wrong thing. Only the fool looses his tongue this way. But it is the wise and the prudent, in love or any discipline, who refrain their lips. No slips of tongue for those who give thought to their ways; no tongues at all for those who needn't prove the silence." Tacit ascent toward, or evidence of, real love, I think, this conversationless comfort; the stillness of silence between two worlds near enough to whisper, ear-to-ear to hear, but with no need or desire to say anything at all. But of course, there were times for words. There's the light.

We treaded over the tram rails, veered left again, then a slight right, and headed southeast through the avenues and streets, catching and throwing glances at one another, then some at the world around—the people passing, cars and cycles and grown adults zipping on upright and neon lit scooters, and all that city noise that posed no threat and had no bearing on our bond of silence. Arm-in-arm once more now, closer and closer, I reeled him in again. In my mind, the only threat to our mood, coming in and at us in warm and nauseating waves, was that obnoxious smell of sewage leaking up from the drains and gutters underground, bringing about sudden scowls, crinkled noses and brows, quick shudders and slight shakes of head, jarring hands over mouths, even small staggers of feet. Before then, I could not for the life of me remember what was missing in the smell of the air in that city. It was the sea, I think. Yes, only sewage indeed, and hot cement, motor oil and exhaust. But that was city life, and so we made our due. By the sea again, by next morning's light, we would make our home.

A little further toward The Marquis now, Bruce slowed our pace by an old brick building. It was Shakespeare Tavern. Bruce read the posted sign nailed upon the door: "TO BE OR NOT TO BE, CLOSING SOON EITHER WAY. AND YES, YOU'LL HAVE IT: FINAL PLAY 'AS YOU LIKE IT.' RUNS 'TIL DEATH OR 'TIL THE TWELTH NIGHT THIS MONTH."

"Huh," Bruce thought aloud, shaking his head in manifest disapproval. "So, another house falls to 'sluttish time,' 'wasteful war,' and 'broils' which have indeed rooted out the merry mason's work."

"Yes, perhaps, but even if the world wore out to 'ending doom,' 'till the judgment,' that poetry will 'live in this, and dwell in lovers' eyes,'" I countered, thankful for all our play-filled nights.

"Not if the world, 'all posterity,' lovers or not, ceases to read the words. There is no record, living or dead, of a word unread."

"My," I thought, "He was right, and nearly there, but only just. For there were words unheard also, and words unsaid, for which no man or woman may ever know, yet they live still." I found my hand clutching my pocket, but I released my grip once more, and returned my hand to his elbow. "Not yet."

Down the lane, through that pinnacle where three avenues met, past the statued square and his favorite car always street-side on display, a little further in, we made The Marquis, entering in to what I knew to be the most magnificent atrium in all the world, and what was, in place and at one time, a founding monument to all we were.

In the driveway, an imposing sense of compression fell over you, as if the low concrete roof were moving slowly downward upon you, leading the mind to believe, perhaps, if it were not for the lower portion of that giant sphere emerging from the roof's center, set over the round and tiered fountain—at the low edge of which a child bent over in a desperate attempt to retrieve, before his fast-approaching mother snatched him up, what I imagined might be all the money he had ever seen in wishing coin—that the world above where you stood would soon close over and crush you forever. A little further, though, in through the sliding doors now, the child, grinning ear-to-ear in his mother's arms behind us, thankful that he was permitted to keep one shining quarter dollar, I faced forward, holding Bruce a little closer but peaking round at him from just behind, trying to read his eyes, his face, his mannerisms for that first-time-seeing sensation. But my eyes, as much as I fought against them, were drawn upward out of my control as we stepped out over the atrium floor.

Given the experience just outside, and at and after the gradual increase in light and space through the entryway lobby, it was, in so many words, a rapturous delight having your eyes lured up and toward the glorious expanse of off-white height, ribbed and skeletal yet alien symmetry, and the natural blue light coming in strong and bright from the skylight at the highest point in the roof's center, mixing as it fell into the soft and serene yellows of the building's interior accents, the whole of it juxtaposing the dimness and the downward moving world you only just escaped. The fullness of that experience just now dawned upon me in an epiphany of sorts, recalling the question of whether or not the architect had planned the whole mental procession from the world outside to the world within: dimness to light, the open but closing in, into the enclosed but opening height. I moved forward again toward the capsule elevators, but my arm caught at the first step. Bruce was motionless, head turned up, mouth gaping, leaning on his cane set behind him now.

"Bruce? . . . Bruce!" I beckoned. He came to.

"I think . . . I think I need to sit down," he stammered, looking a little panicked, but with a sheepish grin. He was sweating. I smiled too, only a little nervous for him.

"Alright, dear, that's quite alright. Here, to the chairs, this way," guiding him to our left where, in the open, there were a set of seats with an end table between. We only sat for a moment, Bruce, sinking down and leaning back, over and again in slow cycles, bringing his eyes to center forward and drawing them up once more, taking in the dynamic once, twice, three times. On the final spell, in such awe, he breathed out, "Oh, my." And I laughed in gay amusement and then stood slowly, gesturing for him to rise as well, and to follow.

"Let's eat something. Are you hungry?"

"I think so. Let's do," he agreed, rising on his cane.

We sat for lunch at the hotel lobby bar, a lunch that lasted all day into dinner, for the conversation. As the time faded toward night, it was like so many other evenings in so many other cities across the world, whereby I knew again that day, in that moment, freshly Stateside, wearily jet-lagged and travel-laden, that there was no place better to dine than anywhere in your home country when just yesterday was spent abroad. The experience, to me, was second only to dining at home, your true home, after a long journey through places, familiar or not, that were far away and thus foreign.

"You ready to go up?" I asked after dessert. He turned sharply to me across the table.

"Where? Up there?!" pointing upward. "No, thank you."

"Come now, Bruce. You aren't afraid of heights, are you?" His honor checked, he sat straighter, ruffling his shoulders and rolling them back, erecting his posture, wrinkling his forehead a bit.

"Well, no, of course not. I just—I mean, are we even allowed to the top?"

"Only one way to find out," I exclaimed, jumping up and pulling him by the hand, skipping away from our table toward the elevators, nodding to our man at the bar to close our tab and cover our meals, meeting his nod in kind and his smile back, taking it in as a familiar wish of luck and good fortune for which in every place, by a thousand house-keeps, stewardesses, servants, table maids, bartenders, butlers, and bishops who knew our story, I was given a share in that common human courtesy that we might together call charity. It was, for me, something to be cherished indeed, and it was what kept me going in days, in hours, in moment-by-moment doubt.

Within the capsule, encased in glass on the atrium facing side, with a typical sliding metal elevator door behind us, well, behind *me*, for Bruce faced the door as far away from the windows as he could space himself in the small capsule. "Bruuuce," drawing out his name in disapproval. He turned his head coyly to see me, head cocked, eyes gesturing, finger turning a whirl, clearing my throat as a mother or a mate might, who wanted to assert her will without words.

"I'm just fine here, thank you . . ."

"Hmph!" I exhaled, crossing my arms as I stomped one foot, shaking the capsule a bit more than I intended.

"Alright, alright, I'm coming round. Don't sink the sky-ship before it ever sets off. There. I'm round. Are you satisfied?"

"Quite," I said smiling and nodding once as the elevator climbed and climbed, story after story, swiftly and silently, and in a moment, we arrived at the top floor, and the memory entered my mind of the first night after our, er—, well, first trip together. Bruce scurried out first and I followed. I could see he was sweating again, having little droplets bead up across his forehead. "Perhaps this wasn't the best idea, so soon after his tumble. Heights challenged him enough in waves," I thought.

"Come now, dear. You're alright. We won't stay long. Just one good glance out over the city," I said, trying to reassure him, rubbing over his back and shoulders. My words were met with no reply. Bruce had made his way around the elevator to a space just in front of the chest-high wall that ran the perimeter of every balcony in an oblong or rounded triangular fashion, with each floor moving up with a smaller circumference so that, when viewed from this height, you could make out the off-white stony walls of the lower balconies, appearing all stacked together, seeming to the eyes as if you were looking down through the ribbed throat of a bony ocean beast, or as if you were peering through a skeletal telescope down into some bright mine that was topsy-turvy, for it was, at this hour, the sun having set now, darker at the top.

Bruce was staring hard over the edge. He looked as if he were seeing through time, through space, through the floor, and into some other world below, leaning gradually toward the edge as if something were drawing him over and down. The sweat, having beaded now in full measure, began to run down his face.

"Bruce?" I queried.

"Eh? Oh, yes, I'm sorry. What were you saying?" he asked, with all his effort drawing his eyes and body away from the edge and the atrium floor below, and toward me.

"The window. Shall we?" I motioned with my eyes, offering out my arm.

"Yes, yes, of course. Let's do," he said, taking my offer.

Arm-in-arm around the balcony we traveled, to that angular window through which we shared together one last glimpse of the city lights, the stadium below all aglow with neon red effervescence. We snapped an admittedly poorly lit photo and walked leisurely back toward the elevator, down and out of it, out of that glorious atrium, through the oppressive driveway, and back into the city streets, where the bustle of the nightlife outside bid us good evening.

Bruce told me later what he was thinking on the ledge on the low wall beside the elevator, as he peered down to—or through—the floor. He said he wondered what it would be like to fall over, or even to jump off that ledge, not for any reason at all to do with ending his life, though he knew he could never survive the fall. He simply wanted to know, to manage that fall, compelled by what logic-defying force he could never understand, for everyone knew it was indeed possible to manage a fall of that magnitude, but it was always and forever impossible to stick the landing. But he wondered most if anyone else in the world, of sound mind, thought the same when on a high floor looking down.

"Eh-hem," I broke in, having shot up my hand at the start of that last thought.

"Yes, my boy. What is it?" the old man inquired.

"*I* have thought the same, on more than one occasion even, and I value my life a great deal more than many I know."

"I see. We are in kind, then, you and I. But know this: you and I have not thought as much on our own, and it is not often an innocent wonder. There are whispers, you know, around all ears, whispers that tempt men in myriad ways. It may not be the mind alone on that ledge, for what better way to destroy a man, than to have him destroy himself?"

"Oh. I never thought of it that way. Do you really think . . . ?"

"Quiet, please. Enough of that. Questions come later. Now, where was I?"

"The night bustle . . ."

We started on our same path back to North Avenue Station, the youths on scooters that were lighted brighter now, whizzed by us, looking odd, I thought, moving down the lanes and avenues in an amusing display of speed and light and nostalgia. But I could see no amusement in Bruce. The light had faded again from his eyes, and he was nearly gone not fifty feet from The Marquis.

"Are you tired, dear?" I lovingly questioned, squeezing his arm, arresting him to a stop.

"Eh? What's that? Oh, no . . . I mean, yes . . . Or, I don't know. Where are we?" stuttering and muttering and looking round as a fresh pack of youths whirred by us.

"Nearly home, dear, nearly home. So no sense in rushing. Let's stay the night. We'll make way at dawn's light." Bruce agreed, but in caution and in that old familiar wariness of spirit. We trekked up to The Marquis, and slept without adventure.

In the morning, at first dawn, we retraced our steps back to the station, again in conversationless contentment. Just down from the park, by the factory, Bruce pulled away and drifted toward the street on our left where there was, parked along the curb, a white convertible. I slowed my pace to see what he was up to. I remembered in that moment, viewing him from some distance, how I liked the way he walked, which is difficult to describe, you know. Perhaps it was an affinity for the peculiar or the distinct or the characteristic charm one notices in any person of particular interest. Bruce stopped beside the car, bent over on the driver side, stood up, walked around to the rear, bent over again, raised, walked to the front, stooped yet again to scan under the car, then over to the passenger side for one final glance beneath.

"What in the world are you doing, Bruce?" I called out with a smirk, shaking my head a little, holding out my hands in fascination.

"Checking for penguins," he replied confidently in that manner of men convinced of not only the rightness of a thing, but its necessity.

"Wha—? But, Bruce, we're not in . . . Never mind," I sighed, shrugging my shoulders, realizing still how futile the talk of geography would be now, and feeling a bit set back at the lapse. "C'mon, we've a ways to go yet," waving him back over to me.

"But . . . we won't be driving?" he asked, still pulling at the passenger door handle.

"No, Bruce, not yet. That's not even ours. We'll take the train to our lot, by the airport. Come now. Let's hurry." In his defense, it *was* a white Jaguar, of the same model and a similar year, no doubt.

53

We crossed the street to the park side, then stopped again at the cross and walk, in front of the factory now, when I caught a glimpse of the most peculiar sight. Walking, or should I say, *waddling* out of the aquarium came five small, flightless birds, coming down the ramp and out into the open air and grassy plane of the courtyard, with the trainers, children, and their parents following all the way, smiling and laughing and making such a fuss about the extraordinary scene: penguins in the city. What a world, and what a surprise that Bruce's caution was confirmed. Even in an American city, with no coast or sea air to smell, warranted it might be, to check under your car before driving away, for penguins. Well, at least in this American city, though I was not convinced Bruce for sure knew where we were at all.

We made the southbound train a short time thereafter, and by chance found two seats together on the crowded car. One stop down, at the change, in the morning rush of people going out and coming in, swapping places and seats for other strangers, an old man in a war hat—a Vietnam veteran cap—stepped through our door and seemed to pause and peer right at us. Well, at Bruce chiefly. The war man seemed to squirm around after making his way slowly into the car. He paced back and forth, cutting glances at Bruce at every turn, nervously it seemed. His hand was feeling over something in his pocket. Then, suddenly, the man stopped and locked eyes with Bruce, and said gravely, "I know you got more than two dollars . . ." I nearly laughed at the charge, but Bruce, wide-eyed, then proceeding to roll those eyes in begrudging agreement, seemed to succumb to that silly conviction as he sat back reaching for his wallet, which I knew he always kept in his front pocket.

"No, dear," I asserted, placing my hand on his. "There is no real need there, not anymore, perhaps there never was to start. Pray, rest. We've a long drive ahead." Bruce nodded and slumped down in the hard seat, giving way gradually to the rattling wheels and the rhythms of the railway world, succumbing to the long staved-off true sleep as slivers of light shined out around the buildings again as the morning sun rose over the cityscape. And just as his eyes set to close, I uttered low and soft in his ear, *"Time to fall, Bruce . . ."*

VI

Captiva

BRUCE AND THE BOAT, AND A COMING TO

I RELIEVED THE MOORINGS, untied the ropes, dropped the motor, and made way for the island. The two-mile-long bridge ran the gauntlet along the east side of the island on our left, disappearing in the distance behind us as we set a north heading through the bay, then through the channel and into the sound, then up and around the pass and down into the bayou and, at last, the boat and I made our approach through a narrow inlet around a cove of sorts, into shallow and mossy waters where it was common to see dolphin run up the stern on either side. At times, the creatures would catch your eye, looking very sentient indeed, rolling and blowing, jumping and flipping, as if they were quite aware of you and aware of themselves, seeming as if they wanted to play, suspecting you might too, or, perhaps, as if they expected a fish from your hand, or maybe a chance at flippered fame like the few who made it out and into the silver pools of aquatic stardom.

Further in, a shadow moved under a dark patch of water as we neared the small and unassuming dock behind the marina. Gray and round with moss on its back, the scarred boulder-like object floated up to the surface. It was a sea cow, grazing leisurely over the kelp forest, looking less sentient but friendly still, in the most stoic and disinterested manner of which classifies entire species of mammals, and what shows itself in personalities of the human kind too. I glanced up from the water's surface and righted our course for docking.

A faint voice echoed through that still air over the quiet marsh as I cut the ship's wheel starboard. "Captain, my Captain," I heard it say. Looking up, I was struck, stunned even, at the sight of the eyes—*those* eyes—so light and so lucid as the noonday sun which, to a man mid-daydream perhaps, might break out from around gray streaks of clouds, opening wide through a pale blue sky, as if a gale suddenly rushed over the horizon at just the moment he was attempting—and succeeding—at making a shape out of the nearest cloud, just to have it whisked away, revealing in a searing epiphany what really gave all the world its shape and size and reality by its blinding but guiding light.

What eyes hers were, seen another way, like a tiger's burning bright through jungle trees which at first sight would halt the pace of even the most seasoned explorer, until he determined whether they were the eyes of a friend or a foe, a tame beast or a wild one, a happy cat or a hungry one. If anyone knows a tiger, such solitary cats can turn on a paw and pounce, shifting from play to prey in an instant, in one swift motion, changing from what we might imagine a peaceful pet, into its true self as a pitiless predator. Many a keeper at the zoo, or a private owner, I suspect, might have come to this conclusion, and not without consequence. What was on this tigress' mind?

She called me Captain, *her* Captain, and what a familiar tone turned. The words rang out in my ears, reverberating between them, listing to-and-fro in my mind, in sync and in rhythm it seemed with the easy sway of the pontoon, so much so that a glaze came over my eyes, whereby I nearly grounded the leisure boat—which is difficult enough to do anywhere—on the shallowest rise of the marsh behind us. Her eyes met mine again after what took all my strength it seemed, diverting my attention away and back to the task at hand, where through a rather frantic tantrum of turning over the ship's wheel—full aft, then port, then starboard again—correcting course once more just in time to ease into safe harbor. I wiped the free beading sweat from my brow as she smiled in my direction, so warm and so friendly and so at ease in a mirth beyond measure, and all at once I realized we were the only two souls aboard that old pontoon. A quietness fell upon the place, and I had time to think.

She said she saw shadows of me in those moments, and those were the hardest times, to see and to know, "There, just there! That's Bruce. That's *him*," and then ruthlessly, without cause and without notice, it seemed that they would fade, as all shadows do, with time, and so quickly then, into all darkness, for I, the real me, would leave, would escape away and travel back off somewhere beyond the rift of this world—of all worlds—to where exactly no one yet knew. But really, deep down, she never expected what would happen next.

"What happened?!?!" I exclaimed again, uncontrollably.

"Calm down, boy. We're nearly there, to the cottage, you see . . ."

Over the sound of the small, thin ripples lapping against the tin pontoons, at the smell of the marsh rife with fish, rising warm to the nostrils up out of the glades beneath, gradually at first, in that quiet moment, now falling full without warning, a terror came over me, a sense of remembrance, of a hot and weighty sentimentality, rolling in and sinking down to the pit of my stomach, like an anchor of ironclad recall settling its yoke, rustling up the sands of some work of the utmost importance, some thought in dire need of remembering, as if there were some thing, perhaps, some Pandora, some panacea, some idea, some construct; to contain, to administer, to grasp; to pick up, or to put back, or perhaps, to take off, or to finish, to finalize; a plan, a destination, a period, a visit, a call, a carrying on, or a coming to. Any doctor might relate, who realized he forgot a step in an invasive procedure, or missed a symptom in a diagnosis, just as he finished his hands at the wash bin, or having just mailed the letter in an era before Mr. Graham Bell's patent. The same thought might run through the mind of a surgeon who, having just sewn the last stitch to close an awful wound, remembered he forgot one operative measure, or left something out altogether, or even left something inside. A worker in any discipline might understand, having just finished a meaningful assignment, still surveying their work in their mind, mulling over all that needed completing, recalling suddenly how all was in fact not done, in order, or even done at all, completely anyway—a line missed, a mark forgotten, a note omitted, a word overlooked where there was no turning back; a test submitted, a plan presented, a symphony performed, a story published—that sharp sense of finality in a thing undone. Though it seemed certain to me, the turn here was to life or death, and not to mere regret.

Such a line of terror through the mind indeed altogether ruined what would have otherwise made for a peaceful end to a short and spirited sea journey, with a hopeful start to the land leg of it. But at that moment, I could only wince and tremor and try to forget, or try rather to remember. The feeling lingered all through, as did some force nearby, one I rather feared—a thing unseen, a thing surreal, *some* thing uncanny, *some* thing on the move, something like destiny arriving in the dark.

The woman behind the words stood, and spoke again,

"Fine work, Captain. Though I thought we might have run aground back there, but only for a moment. All's well, now, of course."

"Oh. Oh, yes, just a slight scare. I just wanted all on their toes and ready to disembark," I averred in a still-perplexed state, surveying the all-but-empty seats around the railings, thinking that even the manatee now looked upon me with pity. I swore I saw it shake its head. "Eh-hem," clearing my throat. "Slow boats, these pontoons, you know. Not much fun for some . . ."

"But fine for us."

"Ya—yes, indeed, for the leisurely sort."

"For those not in a hurry. I quite like the ease of it, and the quiet. Do you know how far we've come?"

"Only two or three miles by now, from coast to cove, you know. Have you been here before?"

"Oh yes, more than you remember. I'm on to the Ship's Store. Care to join me?"

I paused and thought, then yielded to the indefectible draw of her gaze. "I think I might. Have you the time?"

"Half-past three, I think."

"No, no. I meant, have you anywhere to be? I mean, anyone to see?"

"Oh, no, not really. I am right where I want to be. Though, there is the Ship's Store. Come, we better hurry. The light might fade."

Clouds rolled black in the distance over the gulf, and thunder billowed through the deep, signaling an approaching summer storm. The woman was right. Darkness rushed with the wind across sea to shore, and made its approach over the sun just as we made the Ship's Store.

I decided to wait outside, to watch the storm approach while seated at a bench at the edge of the marina, but one still within earshot of the cheerful chime from the bell which hung above the Ship's Store's entry door. An awe-inspiring event, I thought, at each viewing, watching nature's show, so full of familiar smells and sights and sounds—the storm, the main event of any day at sea, when one makes shore in time. She said she'd only be a minute, anyhow. Time enough for the first act.

A line of light flashed in view, startling the nerves, which braced themselves for the anticipated arrival of . . . "What's that?" I thought to myself. Voices from within the store, spirited voices, *her* voice shouting, and a man's in return, a volley of emotion, then low tones, and tears, then sighs to acceptance. The thunder rolled. Then the door's bell, and the man, a large man, burly, hairy, in a workman's jumpsuit, boots, a hard-hat under one arm, both gloves in the other hand, covered in dirt, soil it seemed, from deep underground. He looked long at me—a flash of tunnel lights, the smell of soot, the sound of drills and crumbling earth, shadows so black and work so tiresome blinked through my mind. The man nodded solemnly, placed hat on head and was gone, around the clubhouse and out toward the T-dock. The bell tolled again, and the woman, taking in a great breath and smiling at me as she eased it out and opened her eyes. She stood before me.

"Come, it's time," she said, taking my hand, guiding me up and off to our right, then left down the lane. The trolley passed by us, close on that narrow street, down by the coal built house, the courts on our left, higher rises on our right, then down a path that led through reeds and palms and fronds where gravel turned to sand under our feet, where my cane sank deep, and then, a brown

59

cottage came into view, a cottage by the sea set on its own small plot of paradise.

We hurried inside that cottage by the sea as the black clouds released their stores in steeped gusts and swishing gales signaling those seaside summer showers that tormented that otherwise serene and peaceful gulf coast island town. Though, storms come in waves in any place, I suppose.

She turned the key as the rain fell hardest overhead of where we stood, side by side, huddled thankful under the eaves. She opened that pale blue door and ushered me in with hopeful and excited glances. Through the threshold, music was playing softly in the background, from an old phonograph by the needling and vibrating sounds of it, something instrumental. I shuffled in and made my way slowly down the hall, almost as if I were in a gallery and every work on the wall, or every statue on display caught my eye in a way it might for an art student who had, unfortunately, throughout her studies, only ever made sense of art itself in pictures and through slides and on papers upon which were written a thousand words to describe an experience impossible to encapsulate in any other medium than in reality, in person, an oblivion that same student may take into her retirement, only having that rapturous epiphany, in old age or young, when she at last stood before what she only ever knew in her hitherto two-dimensional imagination. For any student of the past, it might occur the same. One can study the Wailing Wall in history books without ever moving an inch toward emotion, but the experience is very different standing at its base, close enough to feel its warmth, near enough to see its stones which have stood for millennia, and present enough to hear the prayers of peoples subjected for just as long. For me, I was never really anywhere until that moment in that hall, though, next moment, I was back in school.

I noticed a fireplace that was obviously an addition, and a strange one at that for a house this far south, but the sight of it calmed me. She knew. Fully inside now, in what was made out to be the living, or sitting, or parlor room, where the fireplace that would flicker and blaze and crackle, lit the whole place in an amber, warm, and swift-waltzing hue without any actual heat, or mess, or ash. I took in the interior scene, and concluded upon a suspicion that came over me at my first step within, one which survived the gallery. It was, to my chagrin or to my surprise, a house which appeared lifted from another place: the photos on the wall in the foyer, the grandfather clock on one side, an old waist-high banister run over with ferns and air plants and canvased phrases of peculiar sentiment, rugs and throws and what I realized fully now was a digitized, electric fireplace in the low dresser, the curio cabinet filled with well-lit porcelain wares of odd shapes and faces, and curtains of a Celtic variety, all of which were much too ornate for a weekend retreat. Everything in view was foreign, not to me, because it all seemed to mean something to my mind. No, it was foreign to a cottage by the sea. And I was certain, no. 94 was that tune softly filling the room over the rain outside, which pattered upon the skylight now, setting an odd and curious, even enigmatic mood to the whole evening.

This cottage by the sea certainly looked its part on the outside, but it was, from that very first step inside, an enigma in its own right within, as if the setting was at some point taken from another place, another time even, and transposed over this interior space, for what purpose I did not know, then anyway, but I was certain too there was a reason the world within called back some other setting, some ancient space in my mind, in its carefully crafted ambiance and its curated decorum. Plainly, from what was expected but absent, there was no thought of a beach anywhere in that house. It was meant to look like, what was it? Yes, dare I say, a home. This was no summer house, no vacation getaway; it was a home indeed, one away from home, and not at all what one expected in a place like that: wicker chairs and bright upholsteries, glass tables and bamboo wardrobes. No, nothing like that here. Only . . . like the room itself was lifted from another abode, and set down here, for some agenda, yes, a staging of the guard, it seemed, save for that boarded-up dwarf door, rounded on the top, opening down into a cellar or a basement, or, a thoroughfare into a subway or a tunnel. Peculiar . . .

"Tea or coffee?" she asked, her voice like the clap of hands in a dark room where you imagined you were alone.

"Tea, please, and I think I'd like to sit," I answered, staring hard at the little wooden door at the back of the living room, looking altogether perplexed, yet again I presumed.

"Of course," she replied, gesturing to the loveseat by the windows which stood ceiling to the floor and opened to the patio outside. Sitting down, I left room for her on my right, and I waited, hearing the kettle rise, the soft clinking of dishes, and the deep swing of the pendulum on old Grandfather Time down the hall.

Ruthie entered from the kitchen. In that stationed sitting room, we joined together for tea and for a humble lunch of sandwiches and a dainty plate of pastries. Rain fell full over the island. There was no light in the cottage now, save for what danced out of the low-slung fireplace. On the couch, Ruthie sat, having moved my cane to the chair beside us, the tray set in front of us. Rain pattered hard against the window. The digital fire crackled softly behind us. She turned to face me, hands clasped and legs together. I halted my reach for the plate of sandwiches, reading the signal she was sending—"I have something to say"—and consequently rested my hands on my knees and faced her. Made uneasy by her calm, composed demeanor, I tried to calculate the weight of the ensuing conversation. Nothing but silence and an ever-warming smile greeted me, though, and that gaze, as if she peered throughout all time and pierced through all armor any man might slip on over his heart. After a moment staring at her awkwardly, I spoke, "What is it, dear?"

As if these words were an answer to some riddle which opened a sealed tome, or an incantation spoken to lift a spell bewitching her, she nodded her head, reached into her pocket, and withdrew a small metal object. It glimmered and flashed in the light from the fireside—canon fire and flashes, shadow and sound and shimmers of light, an energy from a bygone age emanated all round. The height of that no.94 and the smell of, yes, what was it? N°5 came on full over me in that moment. A platinum ring shined from her palm in the dimness of that parlor. There was "light at evening" it seemed, a pale light at first, from a misted morning or a hazy watch in the night, then a zenith shining through that last cloud dissipating at mid-day, at storm's end, or the brightest moon on the darkest night, where night would seem as day.

A peculiar excitement came over me as I gazed at the object. Its surface gleamed even in the darkness, reflecting everything in the room. I thought something might be revealed through its luster. Ruthie took my hand and eased the ring on my finger. Time seemed to slip and draw, ebb and flow as I felt the coldness of the metal over my knuckle. In that moment, the earth no longer shook, no wind roared, and no fire raged—a stillness, and then a whisper.

"Time to fall, Bruce . . . back in love again."

At those words, an old phrase I once read—"recalled to life"—permeated through my whole being, stemming a rush of endorphins as the now easy yoke of remembrance fell upon me. Like a ship drifting long at sea, I found the shores of home; a dragon long entranced, shaken through to see the scales falling from his eyes; a sleeping giant in his cave, awakened by a master's spell, to the light of morning outside. All this to see for the first time in a great while, the fullness of truth. All this time, *she was my wife.*

"How long have I been gone?" I asked, closing my eyes.

"This bout? Three years off and on."

"My God. And you've been with me this whole time?"

"Of course, my Rose among thorns. 'Where you go, I go,' darling. You knew that. You *always* knew that. My word is good, my promise true."

"Ruthie, my bride." I took her hand, and we embraced.

All was recalled to life in that shadowy parlor from another place, from our northern home: my brief stint at the Board, the Thai jail, my tenure at the college, canons and penguins, cars and capes, high cliffs and desert air, abbeys and atriums, friends and foes, the whole history of experience and, of course, the ever-present pursuer, my sweet Ruthie, my bride. Indeed, every kiss, every night, every caress, every morning, every shadow, every light, every question, every conversation, every taste, smell, temperature, every everything returned to its rightful place. It was a renaissance of remembrance, one to terrify no longer, but to renew all that was once put out of sorts.

"How's the front? The tunnel? What news does Mason bring?"

"Don't think about that now, Bruce. Let's just enjoy our tea, and our time together."

And that we did.

I never forgot a thing after that day, my boy, nothing really important anyway. Though the storm that evening raged still outside, there was I, and I was there, and I was really there, in that moment, and there to stay, until today, it seems, never to return to that vague abyss of seemingly permanent forgetfulness. It was, in so many words, the last light at evening I ever needed.

I sat back, astounded. After a moment of quiet reflection, I asked, "Where is she now?"

"Oh, she's home," he replied with a dreamy glance off into the distance over that hospital retention pond.

"How did you first come to forget? Who was that man, in the Ship's Store? Mason, was it? And what of that hobbit door in the staged house, in the cottage? And what about . . .?"

"Now, now, all will be answered, perhaps some other time. You may visit me if you like, on occasion. I live on the marsh now, not far from here. Ask for me by name at the gate, at The Landing. Now, I really must be getting back. Morning comes."

Indeed, the old man had finished his last sentence just as the light of morning eased out over the horizon line. Clouds were breaking around the rising sun, igniting into wicks burning orange and blue as the great light spread its consuming fire over the eastern sky. We said our goodbyes and the old man hobbled to his car and drove off.

I stood tired at the gravity of the story and, no doubt, at the lack of sleep, yet I was animated by the last look of hope in the old man's eyes. I gathered my things to leave, glancing down once more at the bench as I headed back to the podium. The spider had just come out to repair her web. Below her workings, on a rivet in the middle of the seat, there rested the platinum ring, still and yet shimmering it seemed with a new energy. I reached for it. I turned it over and over in my hand as I collected the remainder of my things from the interior of the podium. On my way out, I paused to examine the ring one last time before departing. Upon the outer rim, two faintly visible crosses were etched on either side, merging in the middle of the metal. An inscription on the inner wall read, *Bruce and Ruthie Rosenthal—Till We or the World Fall Away, Till Death or New Life.*

I imagined these inscriptions the escutcheons of two immortal souls connected in this realm by a force greater than time and space and all other immovable constructs, yes, even Death. Behind them and between them and even before them lived a love so uncontainable, magnificent, and unchanging—rushing, flooding, surging—that it might forever shatter the gates of fear and doubt, fall over loss and the broken, all to furrow out unabated into the landscape of eternity, repairing everything in its wake, even a memory lost. So it was, I imagined.

People were bustling about the hospital as it opened to the business of a new day. I left my post, walking on out over the parking lot, ignorant to all but the morning sun shining bright and strong, talisman in hand, the tale growing long at heart, the road wide and open before me.

VII

Epilogue

A Q&A

I VISITED THE OLD man's, I mean, Mr. Rosenthal's house on the marsh the following week, and I discovered that he was in fact a Dr. Rosenthal, a professor of Religious Studies, or was it Art, or History, or Literature, or some odd consortium of the three, or even four? Anyway, his professorship was in some kind of important and very serious field of study, to him and even to the human race altogether, from what I gathered, yet he talked of it in the lightest of airs. What follows is an account of our interview:

Q: *"Why so many keys?" I asked, taking a seat on the chaise in what appeared to be one of three or even four sitting rooms in that expansive, low-slung but open, single-story mansion on the marsh.*
A: "We bought a place in every city, every city we traveled, that is. And not a big place, mind you, just a cottage or an apartment, you know."

Q: *"Why 'Jack'?"*
A: "Oh, it's just a line from a TV show she thought I might remember. And it is the nickname for one of my favorite writers . . . And,

admittedly, it is my middle name. 'Jackson' in full, though I know it doesn't quite flow, in English anyway."

Q: *"When did you grow the mustache?"*
A: "When I was old enough."

Q: *"What was the boat's name?"*
A: "Oh, yes, *The Empress Evening*. I keep her here, docked at the marsh's edge now."

Q: *"Why that old brown Town Car? You can obviously afford something more, err, like that roaring white Jaguar."*
A: "Some things matter less to some people, as they age, you know. I have no need for a fine, fast car now anyhow, just what will get me here and there. Plus, that was her father's car, and we kept it much like children do: keeping mementos of the past, ones only appreciated with time and age and deep contemplation, and only after their owner's departure."

Q: *"Where is she now, Ruthie, I mean, really?"*
A: "Oh, she's home, as I said. Home at last, but not here, of course."

Q: *"How did this all happen? I mean, how did you first come to forget?"*
A: "It was an awful night. A myocardial infarction. That's what they called it. We were in bed, Ruthie and I, you know, that evening, like so many other evenings, reading together side by side. Different books, of course. She found me convulsing right beside her, you see, when she leaned over to ask me the question of whether or not that coffee shop you see on every corner really took its name from that old whale tale. The paramedics arrived within ten minutes, I was told, but I had stepped out for five of those minutes at least. I was dead, son, by what any machine might read, but I wasn't yet gone. It took three long years recovering, but it all came back, my memory, that is. There are many who are not so lucky. But then, I suppose luck had little to do with any of it.

I was interned in the East, not two weeks prior, and not far from where my story began, but only for a day and a night. I can't help thinking still that my whole life has everything to do with that long loss of time and my short stay in a Thai jail before it. My cellmate was an engineer for a boring company on excavation, but he was not at work for any company that weekend. He was smuggling other missionaries like me, for that was my reason for visiting, and it was my mission for a short time. He smuggled refugees as well, across borders—across continents. He was caught making a surface call. Came up in a city one day, thrown into a country cell with me by nightfall. That was the man I saw at the Ship's Store. He was inspecting the end of the tunnel, the end of our tunnel.

"Well, it was good fortune you two ended up in the same cell."

"Indeed. Good or otherwise, fortune has a teller, my boy, and only he can tell what time can do; only one can tell what time *will* do. And by all accounts, I was in prison at just the right time that weekend, and I came to at just the right time too."

Q: "*Hmm, yes. Well, what's that tunnel business about anyway?*"
A: "There's a storm coming, son, a war, rather, as far as we can see it, and not one waged against flesh and blood, you know; it is a struggle against that other sort, that cosmic kind. Do you take my meaning?"

Q: "*I—I think so . . . I mean, I think I understand. When will it all happen?*"
A: "Oh, soon, though all time may be soon to some. But for us, we are making preparations, you might say, here especially. There's something about this town, my boy, about *this* place, where something will happen. Exactly what will happen, hasn't yet been revealed. But the cogs are moving, the machine on its way, the enemy at the gate, and all, and our little company will need a way out that is out of sight. But enough of this cryptic talk. About you, son, see here, you will be asked to take a side too. Be mindful of that choice. You will see it plainly when it comes. Now, be off, but meet back here in a year's time and I will have something for you, and some instructions, wishes of the last sort, if you take my meaning there

too. I wonder if I'll see the fall again next year . . . Anyway, you really best be off now. There is much to discuss, and you are not yet ready."

As he said this, a knock at the door turned my head across the room.

"Come in," bellowed the old man without ever glancing at the door. Next moment, a party of rather a kaleidoscope of faces and a cacophony of voices flowed and fluttered inside the house: some very distinguished looking men and their wives, some blue collar workers too, and some of all demographics, ethnicities, shapes, and sizes, even languages as I saw and heard them from my seat on the sofa. The old man nodded at me, then toward the door, still open as the last couple waltzed in. I nodded in kind, stood, made my courtesies to the strange council of bodies and spirits so full of wonder and mystery, and I was off, out the door and headed home again, perhaps, to pace and plan and think once more, and to mark my calendar for one year's time from now, thoroughly intrigued at the old man's invitation to return to that magnificent mansion on the marsh, back here, to Dr. Rosenthal, to another tale, I thought, I hoped.

"Oh!" I exclaimed to myself just as I exited the Landing's gate, feeling the cold weight of something small but substantial in my front pocket. "I forgot to give back his ring."